EVOLUTION SHIFT

KURT WINANS

BOOK THREE OF **THE NEW WORLD** SERIES

INDIGO

Livonia, Michigan

Book design by
Blue Harvest Creative
www.blueharvestcreative.com

Story concept by Kurt Winans

EVOLUTION SHIFT

Published by Indigo
an imprint of BHC Press

Library of Congress Control Number:
2017936687

ISBN-13: 978-1-946848-00-0
ISBN-10: 1-946848-00-X

Visit the author at:
www.kurtwinans.com &
www.bhcpress.com

ACKNOWLEDGMENTS

For those of you who have read the first two segments of this adventure, *Pilgrimage* & *Second Moon*, I thank you for returning to enjoy yet another installment of the ongoing saga. There are a few souls who deserve my gratitude for the assistance that they provided, as I would not have been able to complete this segment without them.

Without any doubt, my wife Cathy stands above all the rest as the most important person in my life. Per her norm, she provided the strength for me to carry on with this endeavor when external forces seemed determined to prevent me from doing so. The unwavering faith and patience that she exhibited were an inspiration. Brian met with me regularly to listen, and offer suggestions, as to presenting the storyline within this segment so that it could provoke the intended imaginative thought. Renée was also once again involved in the process by reading through early drafts and commenting on the general shape and flow, as well as how they would be perceived. The polish that was achieved through the various insights of the aforementioned became an important aspect to this completed work.

Thank you all for being there,
Kurt

EVOLUTION SHIFT

CHAPTER ONE

HALLUCINATIONS

His most recent battle had been extremely challenging for Ross, but Janet and Dr. Halley finally managed to break his stubborn high fever. There had been much concern for several hours, as throughout that time they had needed to pour nearly a dozen buckets of ice over Ross's body before his temperature and vital signs returned to normal levels. Once Ross had been stabilized, and then drifted off to sleep, Gabriela, Janet, Aurora, Hank, and even Tori Nobles, took turns watching over him.

Colt assumed the first watch after stating, "I swore a solemn oath many years ago to protect Ross, so respectfully, I will take on the majority of this task. I will not hinder any of you from providing comfort for him, but I must, as part of my own self-preservation, remain close by Ross's side."

The subject was never debated when Janet added, "You know it will be of little use to challenge my husband on this matter. His training as a secret service agent has made him fiercely loyal to the oath of protecting my son."

For the remainder of the day, and then throughout the entire night, Colt never left the side of his former boss. He slept on a few occasions when someone else had relieved him, but never for more than an hour. For those who knew him, Colt's actions came as no surprise. He had stood as a faithful sentinel for Ross throughout the years on ₹-593-ЗυΠ-2-2, but the oath spoken of had occurred long before that on Earth. In all those countless times Colt had never showed any negative emotion, but this situation was different. When Janet came to relieve him for a break just after the first light of dawn, she reached up to wipe a tear from his cheek. Janet loved and admired the way Colt had always taken care of her eldest son, and knew that it was breaking his heart to see Ross in such a precarious state.

A few moments later, after Colt had fallen asleep, Janet heard Ross moan ever so slightly. She moved to his side with a wet towel for his forehead, and then smiled while breathing a sigh of relief when she saw his arm move a few inches under the covers. Privately, Janet had developed an ever growing concern that Ross might never awaken, but kept that horrific thought from Gabriela and everyone else. In spite of his favorable vital signs, Ross had remained motionless while sleeping for over eighteen hours since the fever had broken. Fortunately, Ross's slight arm movement had now made her concern moot.

Suddenly, and with relative ease, Ross rolled onto his side facing away from Janet. Then he unexpectedly uttered, "Jessica, it's time to wake up."

Janet was flabbergasted, and wondered if she had really heard Ross speak or was it simply a hallucination based on her own over exhaustion and wishful thinking.

The answer to her internal question came quickly, as Ross added, "Jessica, wake up! We need to hurry, or we won't have time for breakfast before Grandpa drives us to school."

Janet didn't quite know what to do, so she rubbed her eyes for clarity sake and began to lean in closer.

Then Ross, who was well accustomed to his little sister entering his room to wake him for school, became irritated. With no verbal response from her, Ross increased his tone and said, "Come on Jessica, quit fooling around and answer me. I want to tell you about a really weird dream I had last night."

Leaning back to her former position, Janet realized that she was not hallucinating. However, there was now a new cause for concern over Ross's condition. Although pleased that Ross had spoken three times, with words that had expressed coherent thought, it was disconcerting to her that none of his statements had any actual bearing on the present reality.

She sat motionless through several seconds of awkward silence, and then took a glance around the room to see if either Gabriela or Colt had been awakened by Ross. Neither showed any sign of consciousness, so Janet decided that she would take a chance. Leaning forward once again, she whispered a response of, "Ross, Jessica can't hear you, because she isn't with us."

Ross rolled back over toward the soft voice, and then his eyes instantly grew larger. While shaking his head from side to side, Ross closed his eyes again in the hope of clearing away his vision of Janet. Unfortunately it didn't work, because when he re-opened his eyes, she was still there. Then Ross gulped and, much to Janet's surprise, asked, "Am I dead?"

Janet responded, "No you're not dead, although it was touch and go at times during the last few days to be sure."

"Well if I'm not dead, then this must be some sort of hallucination."

After placing her right index finger upon her lips so that Ross would respond more quietly, Janet asked, "A hallucination, why would you say that?"

"Because you can't possibly be here, you died almost four years ago!"

"Don't be ridiculous Ross, I'm very much alive."

"That's impossible. I remember the day in 1957 when dad told me about the car accident that took you away from us."

Suddenly Janet realized that Ross was correct. Because he apparently believed that he and Jessica were still children living in central rural Texas, he really was having a hallucination. She once again glanced around to see if Gabriela or Colt had stirred, then tried to ascertain the depth of Ross's hallucination. Maintaining her soft tone, she asked,

"You wanted to tell Jessica about a really weird dream that you had last night, would you like me to go get her?"

Ross stared at his vision of Janet for a long moment, and then loudly asked, "Jessica, are you awake?"

Once again there was no response, but the increased volume of his question had been enough to wake Colt. Shifting himself from fully horizontal to a seated position, Colt then stretched and inquired, "What's going on?"

Janet turned toward her husband, and once again used her index finger to keep the room quiet. Then she repeated her question to Ross of, "Do you want me to go get Jessica?"

"I want to tell Jessica about my weird dream, but you can't possibly go get her because you are not real!"

While maintaining her best bedside manner, Janet said, "I understand Ross. If you believe that I'm a hallucination, then you should close your eyes until Jessica comes to wake you?"

With that Ross closed his eyes, and Janet could see his body relax. Colt, who was now standing, shrugged his shoulders and inquired, "What's going on with Ross?"

Janet moved toward him and replied, "This last bout of fever must have triggered something within him, because Ross is having a strange hallucination. I'll wake Gabriela and keep her out of his direct line of sight, but can you do me a favor?"

"Sure, what do you need?"

"We need a young girl who might pass for a childhood version of Jessica to determine the extent of this hallucination. Ross says he wants to tell Jessica about a weird dream that he had last night, so Kristyn could really help us out. Could you please go get her and Natiya as quickly as possible, and explain what is going on?"

"All right, I'll be back in a few minutes."

Upon their return Janet instructed Kristyn on exactly what she needed her to do, and then moved close enough to Ross so that she could hear everything that would be revealed about the dream. Kristyn then began her task by softly pushing on Ross's shoulder and continuously repeating the request of, "Wake up Ross, it's time to get ready for school."

Ross opened his eyes and smiled at the sight of the young girl. For the moment anyway, Janet's plan had worked. Ross immediately said, "Good morning Jessica, how are you?"

"I'm fine thanks, how did you sleep?"

"Great, but I had the weirdest dream."

"Was it scary?"

"Sometimes, but mostly it was just weird."

"Well what happened?"

"I dreamt that when we grew up, we were still best friends. I married Patty and then became an astronaut, and you were a lawyer. Then later on, when all three of us were much older, I became the President of the United States."

"You, the President?"

"Yep, but that's not the really weird part of the dream. When I was an astronaut on a moon mission I met an alien from outer space, and years later he helped some of us escape to another world when it looked like Earth might be destroyed."

"You're right, that is a weird dream."

"There's more. When we were old we got to see mom."

"What do you mean?"

"In my dream, mom didn't die in the car accident. The aliens I mentioned had abducted her and kept her in captivity for a long time."

"They didn't hurt her did they?"

"No she was fine, and she didn't get very much older while she was held captive either. She still looked as pretty as she does in that picture of the four of us next to dad's bed."

"Well that's good, what happened next?"

"The aliens took us to live on a moon in a faraway solar system, and she came with us."

"That sounds nice."

"It was great and I'll tell you more about it later, but for now we need to get ready for school."

Janet had heard enough, and dried the tears in her eyes before advancing to Kristyn's side. Then she softly said, "Ross, everything that you just told Kristyn is true. It wasn't a dream, all of that really happened."

Once again faced with an image of his mother Janet that he thought to be a hallucination, Ross became visibly rattled. Then he looked at the young girl posing as Jessica, and asked her, "Who is Kristyn?"

"I'm Kristyn!"

"No you're not, you're Jessica."

Janet moved closer to Ross, and said, "It's true Ross. This is not 1961, and you are not a boy any longer."

Now looking even more scared by the current moment, Ross stated, "This is not happening. None of this is real."

Janet's bedside manner was beginning to wear thin, so she took a deep breath to collect herself. Then she said, "Ross, if you don't believe us, then just pull one of your arms out from under the covers."

After a reluctant moment, Ross complied with the request. What he saw instantly shocked him back into the reality of the present moment, as he was staring at the frail and wrinkled arm of an old man. After briefly scanning his surroundings for familiar artifacts that could perhaps refute the obvious, Ross returned his gaze toward Kristyn and said, "You're not Jessica, who are you?"

"I'm Kristyn, don't you remember me?"

Then Ross glared at Janet and said, "I'm an old man!"

From her unseen position some fifteen feet behind him, Gabriela replied, "Oh my dear husband. You most certainly are an old man, and you have been acting as stubborn as always."

Janet breathed a sigh of relief when Ross exclaimed, "That sounded like Gabriela!"

Moving to his side, Gabriela replied, "Yes Ross, it's me."

The relief then took hold of Colt when Ross added, "We are all back on Earth, aren't we?"

Now firmly clasping his frail and exposed hand, Gabriela leaned toward her husband and kissed him. Then she replied, "Yes we are Ross, and it's because of you."

CHAPTER TWO

MEMORY TEST

While continuing his recovery, Ross eventually made his way over to the table with some assistance from Colt. Thirsty and famished, he then drank several containers of water and devoured a huge plate of vegetables. A moment later, Aurora rushed through the doorway, and said, "Hey dad! I just spoke with Natiya and Kristyn outside. They said you were awake."

Feeling somewhat stronger and revitalized, Ross turned toward his daughter and replied, "I am indeed, but I was quite surprised to learn that I had slept for roughly eighteen hours."

Gabriela continued to push containers of water toward Ross so that he could fully rehydrate, and then instructed, "Due to your most recent episode of high fever and hallucinations, I think it's a good idea to test your memory."

Ross replied, "How do you plan on doing that?"

"I'm not sure exactly, but there must be something we can think of that isn't too ridiculous."

Aurora then intervened by asking, "Hey dad, why don't you try to relive a specific event for us?"

To which he curtly replied, "Such as...?"

Hoping that he would recognize the difference between his previous time on Earth and the present, Aurora asked, "How about the first time that we rode on the shuttle?"

Ross sighed and said, "That's easy. You and I first rode on the shuttle nearly six months ago. Tori took us up less than an hour after the groups of recruits had all been shipped off to their various destinations."

"Very good dad, but can you expand on that thought?"

As Ross began to weave the tale of the events that had transpired, Aurora nodded as a gesture of confirmation. She had also remembered the words spoken that day, and was relieved that her father's memory seemed to be intact. Then Aurora drifted off into her own accounting of the event.

Tori had led them both to a nearby unused shuttle, and after informing a crew member that she had some people to take on a short ride, the three of them ventured inside with him. Apparently, the pilot seated inside was accustomed to flying at or near full capacity, because he looked up from the instrument panel at the three passengers and asked, "Isn't there anyone else coming?"

Tori then placed her hand on the man's shoulder, and softly replied, "No, it's just the three of us and your crew."

After once again glancing toward the passengers, the pilot had then inquired, "Is this on your authority?"

Without hesitation, Tori had answered, "Yes it is."

The pilot then said, "Alright, what's the flight plan?"

Tori shrugged her shoulders and responded, "Nothing in particular, but please take us up for about twenty minutes."

He had replied, "Alright, take a seat if you're ready."

Seconds later the shuttle was climbing into the sky, and within minutes Ross had said, "The engineering and responsive maneuvering ability of this shuttle are impressive. It reminds me of the jet fighters that I used to fly when I was much younger."

Aurora remembered that at that moment Ross had flashed back to his years as a pilot in the Navy, as opposed to his time in the astronaut program with NASA. Although currently in a craft identical in classification to the three he had flown on during his stint with NASA, even Aurora was aware that there was little else in common with those shuttles.

Ross's comment had obviously intrigued the pilot, as he immediately asked, "You were a pilot? Would you like to sit up front with me for the remainder of the flight?"

Aurora recalled in her memory that the question was rather foolish, but how was the pilot supposed to know that?

After respectfully displacing the co-pilot from his seat, Ross then added, "Fortunately for the passengers and crew, this shuttle also possesses the style and comfort of Air Force One."

No one except Aurora had any clue as to his meaning, but she knew Ross was reflecting on a different time in his life.

A few moments later, Tori moved up toward Ross and asked, "So, what do you think?"

Turning toward her with a boyish grin, Ross replied, "It's wonderful Tori, thank you very much!"

With a return smile, Tori then said, "I'm glad that you like it. Unfortunately we need to turn back now, but we can certainly go on another flight in the future if you want to."

Ross was not about to let such an open invitation slip past him, and Aurora smiled when she remembered that he had emphatically stated, "Tori, I would love to go up anytime the opportunity presents itself!"

Patting him on the shoulder, she replied, "Good, then let's make it happen as soon as we can. If you would like, all ten of you who didn't relocate to another population center can come. As you are now aware, there's plenty of room."

Aurora remembered having become a bit concerned at that moment, because she knew Ross's wheels were turning when he said, "That's a great idea, but I have a favor to ask."

Having reached the same false conclusion as Aurora, Tori replied, "Ross, I'm sorry, but I can't let you fly the shuttle. The process of earning qualification takes several months."

Once again with a rather large boyish grin, Ross replied, "No, although I can imagine that flying one of these would be lots of fun, that's not what I had in mind. I wanted to know if you could take us all to a museum on the next flight. It would mean a great deal to me if I could look upon what had been preserved from the many centuries since I lived on Earth."

Aurora remembered being surprised that her father hadn't even tried to talk his way into flying the shuttle. Then Tori, with a look of concern on her face had said, "I don't know Ross, that's a difficult request to fulfill. Honestly, I would have some concerns about the journey."

Noticing an expression of anxiety on Tori's face, Ross had asked, "So, what exactly concerns you about the journey?"

Tori replied, "Well, a number of things actually, but just to name a few, the distance of the round trip and locating a safe landing spot for the shuttle. You see, the museum facility is nowhere near any coastline or body of saltwater. We couldn't refuel, and we might need to use a portion of our precious fuel searching for a secure place to land."

Looking at the pilot, Ross then asked, "Do you have any thoughts on this topic?"

Glancing back at Tori, the pilot shrugged his shoulders and said, "Tori could be correct about the problem of refueling. I would need to crunch some numbers before I could give you an honest assessment."

Attempting to confirm his suspicion, Ross then pressed with, "When was the last time that you flew to the museum?"

The pilot had looked surprised by the question, but then remembered that he was speaking with someone who had only just arrived a few weeks prior. He answered, "I have heard of the facility, and studied some of the historical disc recordings that reveal what's inside, but I have never been there."

Ross replied, "You too? Hasn't anybody been there?"

Tori then interrupted by adding, "Ross, the historical disc recordings have made it easier than venturing to the museum, so no one that I know has ever been there. Besides, according to our records, the museum facility and surrounding area have been completely abandoned for a long time."

Aurora had remembered asking the obvious question so that her father wouldn't need to when she inquired, "How long has it been abandoned?"

Tori then answered quite calmly, "It's been at least four centuries by now."

The vivid memory of the deflated look on her father's face at that moment saddened Aurora, but then she smiled at knowing that the situation had eventually been rectified.

Snapping back into the reality of the present moment, Aurora could see that Gabriela was now visibly more at ease. Ross was obviously feeling much better, and had proved that his memory of different decades within his life was intact. Then looking toward Ross, she said, "Thanks dad, I'm glad that you remember how fun that first flight was."

ᚢ

CHAPTER THREE

WHEELS IN MOTION

Having satisfied Gabriela and Aurora via the recounting of events they had chosen to test his memory, Ross turned his reflection toward those first days and weeks after his return to "New Earth". Although six full Earth months had passed since they had completed the voyage from ₹-593-ʒπ-2-2, for Ross, it seemed like yesterday. The memory of events leading to the first shuttle flight that he had discussed with his wife and eldest daughter were crystal clear as he quietly reflected upon them. Ross, and the other ninety-nine recruits within the group that he led, had been tasked with a specific and daunting challenge. If managed properly, the intended plan could help to ensure the longevity of the human population on this particular marble in space. In spite of facing unfavorable odds, a reality often experienced throughout his life on two different worlds, Ross confronted them willingly. By doing so, he also vowed to make every effort possible in order to succeed.

With help from several others, Ross had successfully set the wheels of the gene enrichment program in motion just a few days after he and the recruits had landed. Assisted by Tori Nobles, one of the administrators of the surrounding population center, Ross began the operation with phase one. That aspect required use of the same vast communication system Tori had employed to inform Earth's current population about the surprise survival and arrival of off-world humans, and the alien species that was responsible for bringing them back to Earth. Now their message was of a different scope, as Ross and Tori informed each global population center of the program and its intended specifics. That would include the eventual distribution of recruits for very specific intents and purposes.

Upon their arrival from ₹-593-ʊπ-2-2, the alien vessel transporting Ross and his group had assumed a low orbital path above "New Earth". After completing a few observational revolutions, a specific landing site was then determined based on a recommendation from Ross. Throughout the course of those orbits, Ross had paid close attention to the planet surface below. Having been well versed in planetary geography from the days of his youthful education at Annapolis, and then via the practical application of global travel associated with the Navy, NASA, and in political circles, it had been easy for Ross to notice the alterations of continental structure caused by the asteroid apocalypse. In some cases the changes were quite dramatic, and while peering out the observation window, with Aurora by his side, Ross had verbally listed the specifics of said alterations to her.

Beginning over the southern hemisphere, the first thing Ross noticed was a source of light near the eastern midpoint of what he knew as New Zealand's south island. The shape and size of the island, as well as that of the neighboring north island, were slightly different than he had remembered, but it was definitely New Zealand. Another light source soon came into view along the southeastern coast of Australia, and that portion of the continent also had a different look to it. At that time he was unaware of the fact, but Ross now understood that the cause of those subtle alterations had been coastal submergence as a byproduct of a dramatic rise in the global ocean levels. Upon closer inspection, Ross believed that the location of the new light source was slightly inland from where Australia's largest city of Sydney had once stood. When Southwestern Australia then came into view, it was obvi-

ous that the region had been far less fortunate. Ross could only theorize, but it was logical to assume that the obliteration of the land mass
surrounding Perth, and the deep azure blue water that now occupied
the area, had resulted from a massive impact.

Crossing high above the Indian Ocean to the west, another light
source was then clearly visible within the southern extremes of the
African continent. On the opposite side of the Atlantic Ocean, South
America revealed two more sources of light. Upon the eastern shore, in
the general vicinity of Brazils Rio De Janeiro or Sao Paulo, there were
significant signs of habitation. To the west, over the massive Andes
mountain range, another coastal site possibly near what had once been
Santiago Chile shone nearly as brightly.

Ross had remembered receiving a telepathic message from his
old alien friend as to their intended orbital path, and had then asked,
"Aurora, are you getting all of my observations down?"

She had been succinct with her mildly irritated reply of, "Yes dad,
I'm writing all of it down."

With a glance in her direction, Ross had then retorted, "That's
good. According to our friend, we won't be going over the same ground
again. Each of the upcoming orbits will take us further to the north,
and we should be over the southern coast of Asia very soon."

As if on cue, the southeast coast of Asia, at the western reaches
of the vast Pacific Ocean, then revealed another light source. As one
would reasonably expect, a sizeable population center existed along the
newly defined southern coast of China. Although nearly half of the low
lying land mass no longer existed, there were also visible signs of life in
India. Another of the large and deep impact sites was then clearly visible, with azure blue water now covering much of what had been Saudi
Arabia. North Africa claimed a presence with a light source within the
southern section of all that remained of Egypt. Then a second source,
along the extreme western reaches of the continent, suggested something in the vicinity of Senegal. After passing over the central Atlantic
and the southern portion of the Caribbean Sea, the strip of land once
known as Central America came into view. Although not as intensely

lit as the previous sightings, a light source was discernable along the west coast of Costa Rica or Nicaragua.

A short time later, another trip over the Pacific revealed that the sprawling mega city once known as Tokyo Japan had not been completely snuffed out. Much of central Asia lay still in the darkness, but there was a clearly recognizable source of light along the eastern shore of the Black Sea. The southern portion of the European continent was then viewed for the first time, and a settlement existed somewhere along the former coast of Portugal. Reaching North America, Ross spotted what would be their eventual landing site as they flew high above another large azure blue water impact site and the newly defined coast of Texas. Ross remembered that as their series of orbits reached more northern extremes while passing over the Pacific, he had inquired of Aurora, "How many locations of habitation have we identified?"

She had then responded more congenially, "My count is fourteen at this point."

Their final crossing high over the land mass of Northern Asia and Europe had revealed no additional sources of light, but then the British Isles came into view. Although a large swath of seawater had encroached from the east via the mouth of the Thames, and blanketed the portion of England where London had once been, all was not lost. To the northwest, perhaps in the region near Liverpool or the border of Wales, a large source of light could be seen.

Reaching North America once again, no source of light could be seen along the eastern seaboard. The previous pass had revealed that Florida, and similar low lying areas within the southeastern region of the United States, no longer existed. That sad news was compounded on the second pass. The entire high population corridor from Boston south to Washington D.C. that once housed millions upon millions of people was now void of any sign of life. Dawn lighting within the region revealed a large impact site that was now filled with sea water. The massive crater altered that section of the coast dramatically, and in so doing, had probably provided most inhabitants of the area with a quick yet horrific demise. Moving again into the darkness below, their orbit reached the northwest coast of the continent. That location revealed one final beacon of light that appeared to be nestled in the area of Vancouver within the former western Canadian province of British Columbia.

The memory of their final orbit above Earth was crystal clear, and Ross had stated, "That brings the total to sixteen."

Aurora had confirmed the count by adding, "That's the figure I have dad."

The information obtained by Ross and Aurora during those orbits had been confirmed by Tori Nobles before phase one of the program had been implemented. Within the course of a preliminary discussion about logistics, she had said, "We are aware that a total of sixteen population centers, including this site, exist at various locations around the planet."

Focused solely on the selection process, the second phase began. Small ethnically diverse groups would need to be assembled from the pool of viable reproduction candidates, and that process would include ensuring that each group contained at least one of the twenty youthful Mayans supplied by the King. For the groups that would have two Mayans within them, it was necessary to ensure that both a male and female were represented. Within the fifty-three males, and forty-three females, that comprised the collective pool, only six would remain at their current location. Of those who would stay with Ross, Gabriela, Aurora, and Janet, the four non-reproductive recruits that rounded out the one-hundred person manifest, the selections were relatively easy to define.

Aurora had been emphatic that her husband Tikal, the twenty-first Mayan on the manifest, would remain by her side. After all, the man had been fully prepared to fight to the death for her hand back on his home world. Then he willingly traveled through the vastness of space for six weeks from ₹-593-ℨ∪π-2-2 to Aurora's birth planet of Earth. Although she had no problem with her husband impregnating several other women to help enrich the dying gene pool of Earth, Aurora felt that she had the right to demand that he return to their dwelling every night and sleep next to her.

The second selection was blatantly obvious as well, but Janet removed any lingering doubt when she announced, "My husband Colt must also be part of this group."

Their young son Hank would need to remain with them, so half of the six member group was therefore pre-determined. As the only other child present on the six week voyage to "New Earth", Kristyn had developed a strong friendship with Hank. It was decided that the interest of both youngsters would be best served by keeping them within the same group, so Kristyn's mother Natiya also became an obvious addition. With that, only one spot of the six person group needed to be filled.

Brittany Cooper, whom Janet had originally met while in captivity aboard the alien deep water vessel, asked if she could be the final member of the group that remained. Janet had been solely responsible for recruiting the cute and curvy young woman from Montana as a participant into the program, but she also had no intention of placing Brittany in a group that lived anywhere near her husband Colt while pursuing the gene enrichment endeavor. In simple terms, Janet didn't want her husband to impregnate anyone that she knew more than casually, and felt the younger woman's obvious temptations were just too great to resist. Aurora possessed similar reservations with regard to her husband Tikal, and promptly agreed with Janet's assessment. Therefore, Brittany was denied of her request and subsequently became a member of the group destined for the southeastern coast of Australia. Both Janet and Aurora felt that if Brittany could somehow manage to entice either Colt or Tikal to mate with her from the opposite side of the planet, then she deserved some credit for her effort.

As four of the five recruits already chosen to remain at their current location possessed either North American or Northern Asian heritage, someone possessing a broader ethnic diversity was needed to help Tikal round out the group. Well aware of that fact, Ross said, "I believe that we should select a woman of either South American or African heritage. Although the group does contain the fresh infusion of Mayan blood from Tikal, it requires additional balance."

Aurora responded, "I certainly understand your point about the ethnic need in this group dad, but why a woman?"

"Well, mainly it's due to Hank and Kristyn. It's logical that they must remain within this group, but they are of little help genetically at the present time. Both of them are several years away from being able to reproduce, and even though you and Janet will remain here, by your own admission, you are not viable candidates either. That means Natiya is the only female currently available for childbearing in this group of recruits. You can't possibly put all that pressure solely on her, so another woman must be selected to help balance things out."

"As usual dad, you make a strong case. Do you have a particular person in mind?"

"Not specifically, but I do know that one of the young female Peruvian runners is on the manifest."

"Yes, I know the woman you mean. That's a very good suggestion dad. Let's place her in this group and consider it to be complete."

Once the entire selection process for the other fifteen groups of six individuals had been finalized, Ross and Aurora could then move forward with phase three, or the distribution, of the assigned members. That was when they first learned of yet another fantastic technology that had been developed by the current residents of Earth, and because of it, the process of distribution became much easier than Ross originally thought it would be. The ninety remaining recruits were sent via flying shuttles to the fifteen other population centers around the globe. The shuttles were large enough to carry twenty people in addition to the crew of four, could fly at high or low altitude with reasonable speed, and were fueled simply by using salt water from the ocean. All the pilots had to do when in need of more fuel was to belly land on the ocean and refill the tanks.

Tori stood with Ross and Aurora as the boarding process began, and joined them in the gesture of shaking the hand of each recruit. Three groups of six boarded each of the five shuttles that would be used for the endeavor, and then Ross saluted the members of each flight crew before liftoff. Seconds after the last of the recruits had departed for their assigned destinations, Tori asked, "Now what can we do to facilitate the efforts of phase four and five?"

Ross was quick to respond, "Well, working in reverse order, phase five is critical and will require a delicate touch. Although much of the baseline information won't be available for several months, meticulous record keeping will be required. In order to ensure the spreading of a healthy gene pool, each set of parents for the new offspring must be known without exception. It's the only way to avoid the potential problem of future generations reproducing with others who share a close common ancestry."

"I understand. We can't create a larger problem."

"Exactly, as it would defeat the entire purpose of the fresh infusion of human DNA into the current population."

Aurora then asked, "Alright dad, that's perfectly clear, but what are your thoughts to facilitate phase four?"

"There's not much that we can do because phase four is, for the most part, beyond our control. We should respect those involved, and give nature time to take its course. Each recruit, as well as those of the appropriate age group in each population center, know what needs to be done in order to assist in saving the gene pool. With that said, the process becomes more about natural selection and then the most basic of human instincts as opposed to anything else."

$$\xi$$

CHAPTER FOUR
MUSEUM PIECE

Within a few weeks after the initial shuttle ride for Ross and Aurora, Tori provided them with a wonderful surprise. She had always maintained a desire to visit one of the planets few remaining museums, but had never seriously considered that such a trip would be possible. That belief suddenly changed when she once again met with the same pilot who had offered Ross the co-pilots seat. He informed Tori that after completing and double checking all the number crunching associated with passenger load and fuel consumption, the round trip flight was possible if certain concessions were made. That conversation provided Tori with the additional motivation she needed, and she knew that Ross and his core group would want to join her.

On the morning of the flight, Ross and the nine other members of his group eagerly awaited their chance to climb aboard for the exploratory adventure. Among them was Tikal, who after a brief period of uncertainty, had dealt with the space flight from ₹-593-ᴣυπ-2-2 quite nicely. For this flight his initial posture was much more relaxed, as both Aurora and Ross had assured him that it would be very short in comparison.

Tori had brought along seven members of the scientific community that expressed a desire to explore what had been neglected for roughly four centuries, so there would be a total of eighteen passengers. When faced with that number, the pilot said to her, "Why didn't you inform me that you were bringing so many people?"

"Is it a problem to have more than I expected?"

"It could be. Very little margin for error exists, because, as you already pointed out, there is no place to refuel between here and where the museum facility is located. We must be cognizant of the total weight that we have on board."

"Do a few extra people really make a difference?"

At that moment, the pilot decided to add another safety concession to his previous list by leaving two members of his crew behind. He knew that shedding the weight would help with the fuel consumption rate, and those crew members were not actually needed for flying purposes. A moment after liftoff, he announced, "The flight to the museum will take longer than the distance would normally require, because I will be cruising at low speed and altitude for maximum fuel efficiency."

Tori then asked, "How long do you think it will take?"

"Probably just over three hours each way."

Throughout the vast majority of the flight, Ross had been gazing out the window for any landmarks that might be recognizable. For the most part the topography was flat and dry, but then he saw large mountains looming in the distance. As the pilot began to slow and search for the exact location of the facility, Ross realized where they were. Then he turned toward Gabriela and the others, and stated, "I can't believe it, but it looks like we are going to land in the mountains of what we knew as Colorado."

Gabriela asked, "Colorado? Are you sure?"

Colt looked out the window for a moment in an attempt to verify Ross's claim, and the identity of their destination suddenly occurred to him. Turning to Ross, he said, "If we're going where I think we're going, then the location makes perfect sense for use as a museum."

The pilot finally located the landmark that the historical disc recordings had referred to, so he began final approach. After setting the shuttle down on a flat area a few hundred yards from the abandoned entrance, he opened the hatch so that the passengers could disembark. Moving briskly toward the entrance, Ross and Colt noticed that the words were still faintly visible upon the identifying arch. Staring at each other, they simultaneously realized they were the only two people in this group of twenty that knew of the facilities former purpose. Then Ross exclaimed, "This is truly unimaginable. Somehow this place has withstood everything for twenty-six centuries!"

Before Colt could reply that they were indeed at the location he had suspected, Tori said, "Ross, I'm not familiar with that word before mountain, can you pronounce it for me?

Ross replied, "It's Cheyenne, the name of this mountain fortification. Now come on, let's all take a look inside."

One scientist intervened by asking, "You know what this place is don't you? Have you been here before Ross?"

Turning toward the woman, Ross smiled and said, "Yes. I have visited the Cheyenne Mountain complex several times, and Colt was actually with me on a few of those occasions."

Tori then said, "Well that's good news for the rest of us, because the two of you can lead us through the facility."

For several hours the group cautiously moved about within the complex, but no sign of human skeletal remains were ever seen. On occasion Colt would look at exhibits portraying life during the centuries after the asteroid apocalypse, but he mainly focused on searching out potential threats or danger.

While on point roughly thirty feet in front of the group, Colt peered around a corner and suddenly stopped in his tracks. As Colt gazed with wonder at the exhibit now directly in front of him, Ross picked up on the familiar posture of his old friend. Without any need for clarification, Ross quietly said, "Everybody stop right where you are, Colt sees something that might be a problem."

After several seconds of everyone collectively holding their breath, Colt turned to them and said, "Ross, there is no danger that I can see or hear, but you have got to look at this!"

"What is it Colt?"

"It's another exhibit, but nothing else that we have seen today can begin to compare with what I'm looking at."

Advancing to the side of his old friend, Ross agreed with the sentiment as he couldn't believe what lay in front of him. When the remainder of the group advanced to join them, Ross gulped and asked, "Colt could you please read whatever is on that plaque so that everyone can hear?"

"No problem Ross. Just let me clean it off first."

"Thank you."

Still quite awestruck, Colt moved forward roughly ten feet and dusted away centuries of cobwebs and dirt from the plaque. Then before beginning to read aloud he turned and said, "Well, it's obvious that the spiders have survived all these centuries."

Another of Tori's scientists exclaimed, "I'm sure many species of life other than humans were able to evolve by adapting to their new environment and survive extinction!"

Ross replied, "That's very well said doctor, and I agree with your assessment. Now Colt, if you please."

Colt turned back to the plaque and began, "This exhibit contains artifacts saved from the Oval Office of the White House in the United States of America's Capitol City of Washington D.C. Each item was obtained during the final desperate days leading up to the asteroid apocalypse which began on August 24, 2022 A.D."

Aurora couldn't help herself, but no one around her seemed to mind as she blurted out, "This is beyond amazing!"

Ross understood her sentiment completely, and added, "It most certainly is. I wonder who was responsible for this."

As Ross and Aurora began to study the exhibit with questioning eyes, Colt asked, "Should I continue?"

Aurora responded, "Sorry Colt. Please continue."

"The contents once belonged to Ross Martin, who as the forty-fifth President of the United States, looked to the stars beyond our technological limitations and helped to provide humanity with a fighting chance to stave off extinction."

Suddenly Tori blurted out, "Ross, is that you?"

Turning to see his bewildered new friend, Ross calmly replied, "Yes, but that was in a different and distant lifetime."

"Indeed. Well, let's add that to the list of subjects we can discuss later. As for now, the plaque says you were the President of the United States. So what does, or should I say did, that mean?"

Janet chimed in and said, "Tori, it means that for a few years Ross was one of the most powerful people on Earth. He became the elected leader of vast amounts of territory that included the land that we are currently standing on and the area of the population center where we all live."

With a sigh of irritation, Ross said, "Calm down mom. I know that you're proud of me for my former accomplishments, but please leave them in the past where they belong."

Colt reentered the conversation by saying, "Ross, there is one more passage on the plaque."

"Alright Colt, we might as well hear the rest of it."

The question that had already surfaced in the minds of Ross and Aurora was then answered, but with an interesting twist. Colt read on, "These effects have been dedicated by the surviving descendants of both the Ross Martin and Dennis Strickland families."

With understandable excitement in her tone, Aurora blurted out, "Oh my God! That means that mom, Rachel, and the rest of the family survived after we left!"

Ross gulped with utter astonishment, and then quickly pointed out, "No Aurora, there is no proof of that. Now please get a hold of yourself."

"But dad, the plaque says..."

He cut her off by adding, "I heard what the plaque claims Aurora, but surviving descendants doesn't specify who lived or died!"

Looking back at the exhibit, Ross recognized an item very dear to his heart. Propped up against the wall, with a torn, faded, and crusted over red ribbon attached, was the fishing pole that he had cherished since his youthful days in Rumley. The message of the plaque, and the fact that the fishing pole was within the exhibit, certainly implied that some member of the Martin family had survived, but there was no way to identify who that person, or persons, were. Ross had given the fishing pole to his grandson Luke scarcely more than an hour before departing Earth in the alien transport, so perhaps he had somehow ensured the artifacts safety in this location or the Strickland family shelter. Not that it really mattered how it was done, because anyone who had survived would have now been dead for twenty-six centuries.

After a moment of contemplation over that prospect, Ross turned toward Tori and candidly asked, "Do you or any of the scientific team have an issue with me retrieving my old fishing pole?"

She made eye contact with everyone in the room, but there were no visible or verbal objections from any of them. With arms then extended to her sides, Tori shrugged her shoulders and responded with, "I can't begin to understand the magnitude of what all of you must be experiencing at this moment, and I hope that you will openly discuss it with me and our scientists at a later time. As for now, I don't think anyone would blame you for wanting to remove a few artifacts of your century from this long forgotten exhibit."

Looking at each of those who had come with Tori on the adventure, Ross nodded and replied, "Thank you."

That was all Colt needed to hear, so he quickly asked, "Ross, would you like me to get the fishing pole for you?"

"Thanks Colt. That would be great."

"Is there anything else you want while I'm in there?"

"Yes. Could you please get the American flag? The two flags that made the journey from old Earth to our former home moon and back have a pre-determined purpose, so we can use this one to educate Tori and everyone else about Colorado, Texas, and your home state of Nevada."

Once retrieved, Hank then cared for the fishing pole while Ross and Colt respectfully folded the flag into a triangle of aged off-white stars with a badly faded blue background. Then, after saluting the flag, Ross asked, "Aurora, could you please watch over this for me, and keep it as safe as you have done so splendidly with the other two?"

Accepting of the challenge, she said, "Most definitely!"

Intrigued by the ritual she had just witnessed, Tori silently added the event to her ever growing list of things she would have Ross explain at a later date.

Moving on, the group soon came upon a chamber which was significantly larger than any other portion of the complex. Ross and Colt instantly knew where they were, but no one else had any clue. Although no longer in use by the time of Ross's presidential administration, the control room had served for many years prior to that as the nerve center for America's former nuclear missile defense system. Fortunately, Ross knew that explaining the need for such a control room before the apocalypse of 2022 may not be in the best interest of those now residing on the planet. The subject matter was delicate to be sure, and Ross understood the need to give it considerable thought before disclosing his knowledge of that aspect of the human endeavor to anyone.

Emerging from the vast network of tunnels, the fresh mountain air was an instant reminder to the group of how stale the air had been within the old Cheyenne Mountain complex.

Shielding her eyes from the sunlight, Tori said, "I'm glad that we came on this trip. I learned some things about our history that were never mentioned on the historical disc recordings, and exploring this long forgotten facility was fun."

Ross replied, "I agree. It's fortunate that your ancestors had the foresight to create those discs for educational purposes, but it's also a shame that so much human history had simply been omitted to eventually become forgotten."

Then young Hank interjected and reminded all those present of what else had already apparently been forgotten. He said, "I thought there were many interesting things for all of us to look at, but to me, the best part of everything that we explored today was the exhibit for Ross. Just think about it. We all learned that our family might have a distant relative living somewhere on this world."

CHAPTER FIVE

FLYING ON VAPOR

Before engaging the engines for the return flight, the pilot and co-pilot performed a standard pre-flight check. When asked for a reading of the fuel status, the co-pilot gulped and quietly replied, "The gauge reads forty-eight percent."

The pilot snapped his head to the right and peered into the other man's eyes. Then he asked, "Did you say forty-eight?"

Nodding positively, he replied, "Yes sir, forty-eight."

Fortunately for the flight crew, none of the passengers had heard the quiet exchange, or noticed the concern on the face of the pilot. They were all quite busy discussing what had been seen and learned inside the confines of the museum.

Leaning slightly to his right in an attempt to further secure their secrecy, the pilot asked, "Are you sure? Maybe the gauge isn't reading properly."

After lightly tapping the gauge with his finger, and then running a quick, but significantly more scientific diagnostic of the instruments, the co-pilot quietly replied, "Everything checks out sir. Our fuel is definitely at forty-eight percent!"

"That's strange. I know that we had the range at slow speed to cover the roundtrip distance. We must have used more fuel than I thought we would while searching for this facility."

"What are we going to do? Should we leave some of the passengers here, and then come back to get them later?"

"No, I don't think that's a viable option. There is no way we could make it back here before dark."

"Then we could come back at first light."

"That would be possible if those we left behind had provisions of food and water, but we didn't bring any with us."

"Alright, then what's your plan?"

"I think we can still make it back home with forty-eight percent if we fly a slow direct course. We will definitely be cutting it close, but I don't believe that we can pursue any other option."

Having mutually agreed that was their best course of action, the shuttle soon began a gentle rise into the sky. After setting a direct course for their population center, the crew maintained a vigilant watch on the fuel gauge.

Ross, having developed a keen eye for such things during his many years as a former pilot and astronaut, had noticed the co-pilot tapping the gauge on the instrument panel. His gut instinct also informed him that the ensuing quiet discussion with the pilot could be a sign of a potential problem on the flight deck. It was not Ross's place to discuss the matter publicly among the other passengers, nor would it serve any productive purpose in creating concern by doing so, but the body language of the two men seated at the front of the shuttle revealed their collective discomfort. While maintaining a well-practiced poker face, Ross inwardly prepared himself for a surprise element to the return flight.

During the early moments of the flight, Ross, with Hank and Kristyn on either side of him, had informed all who would listen about the fishing pole he received from his grandfather all those centuries before. Then he provided them with a history lesson about how each of the stripes on the flag represented one of the original thirteen colonies when the United States came into being. As for the stars, they represented the growth of the nation, as each signified one of the eventual fifty states, including Colorado.

Well over an hour later, when many of the passengers had fallen asleep, Hank moved toward the flight deck. Unable to fight back his nearly always inquisitive nature, Hank wanted to take advantage of the opportunity that had presented itself. His goal was to learn all that he could from the flight crew about how the shuttle operated. Ross seized the same opportunity for a private discussion with Tori. Looking into her eyes with serious intent, he said, "Tori, I need to speak with you about something that is rather delicate."

"Sure Ross. What's on your mind?"

"Your assistance with the first three phases of the gene enrichment program has been tremendous, but now I think it's time for you to consider your role in phase four."

"I thought you said that we couldn't do very much to influence phase four."

"That's true from a logistical standpoint, but I'm talking about your actual participation."

"Excuse me!"

Sensing that he had struck a nerve, Ross calmly said, "Now don't get offended Tori, but I think you know what I mean."

"It sounds like you want me to have a child."

"Yes, but actually, more than one if possible."

"Now you want me to have more than one?"

"Yes Tori. Think of the long term benefit. Your children could be a great addition to the program."

"Ross, are you asking me to mate with you?"

While smiling at the idea that Tori had actually believed that to be possible, Ross replied, "Not at all. I mean, thank you for the sweet thought, but at my age I'm not even a candidate for such an activity."

"I understand. But wait, if not with you, then who?"

The flight crew was unaware of any conversation in the main cabin, as they were busy answering all the questions brought forth by Hank. They were happy to do so, as the young man was pleasant with his inquiries and seemed to understand all the information that was given to him. Each of the gauges, and their purpose, with the exception of the one that displayed available fuel, were discussed at length. While maintaining his fixation on the pressing matter of the fuel numbers, the co-pilot suddenly exclaimed, "Look. I can see a faint line of blue water at the coast!"

Squinting while scanning the horizon, and then nodding with concurrence, the pilot replied, "Yes, I can see it too."

Then Hank added, "So can I."

After asking Hank to please return to an empty seat, the pilot quietly inquired, "What's the gauge read?"

The co-pilot, after ensuring that Hank had moved away, replied, "Six percent sir, I think we're going to make it."

"Well we're not there yet, but we do have a chance."

For the next several agonizing minutes, the coastline and precious fuel supply of the salt water it provided seemed to remain at a constant distance from the shuttle. Unfortunately, the fuel gauge responded differently. Already deeper into the red zone than either pilot had ever experienced, the number dropped to five, and then four.

The co-pilot then asked, "What do you think sir?"

"I think it's going to be very close, so let me know the second we get fully over the water!"

A few moments later the co-pilot looked down at the wide sandy beach, and then while breathing a sigh of relief said, "Just a few more seconds' sir, and you can land."

Glancing at the gauge that now read two percent, he replied, "Good. I think that we're flying on vapor."

Seconds later his thesis was proven correct as he turned left for a landing parallel to the beach. Now starved of even the vapor he had spoken of, the engines failed. Fortunately they were less than one-hundred feet off the water, so they glided in for what most would believe was a textbook refueling.

Once fully refueled, the flight crew inquired if Hank would like to witness the takeoff and landing procedures. Then the shuttle made the short hop over to solid ground so that everyone could disembark.

While retrieving his much younger brother from the flight deck, Ross offered his thanks to the crew for their effort. Believing that he had been the only one of the passengers to hear and feel the engines suddenly shut down a short time earlier, Ross winked and quietly added, "And with plenty of fuel to spare."

CHAPTER SIX

UNSTABLE CONDITION

Five Earth months had passed since Ross and the others had embarked on their adventure to the museum facility, but in the present moment, Janet's thoughts centered on what had just transpired. Although Ross had come through his recent ordeal, Janet pondered the possibility of future hallucinations.

Throughout the six months since the group of recruits under his leadership had arrived on Earth, Ross had been slowly slipping away. His episodes of poor health had unfortunately become much more frequent and intense during the past month, and the durations of those episodes were longer as well. Now there was the new concern of a worrisome symptom that had magnified those medical difficulties. Ross had hallucinated that he was a young boy living in Texas having a weird dream about multiple events that had actually transpired throughout his life. Simultaneously, he believed that it had not been a hallucination, but somehow seeing, and then conversing with, his supposedly dead mother was. In simple terms, Ross had hallucinated living through a terrible dream within the context of supposedly having a pleasant dream.

While leading Kristyn away from Ross, Janet smiled at Natiya who was waiting for them in the doorway. Once they were all outside, Janet said, "I would like to thank you both for what Kristyn just did to help us."

Looking up, Kristyn asked, "Is Ross going to be alright?"

With a quivering tone, Janet replied, "I don't think so honey. Ross is very sick, but we will keep him as comfortable as possible. You did a great job of pretending to be his sister Jessica, and because of that help I can discuss exactly what happened to him with Dr. Halley."

Natiya, while gently rubbing her visibly pregnant belly, then said, "Janet, please keep us informed about Ross, and let us know if we can do anything else to help."

"Thank you Natiya, I will. Now, how are you feeling?"

"I feel really good thanks, and Dr. Halley informed me just yesterday that everything is alright with the baby."

"That's good news, how far along are you?"

"I'll be twenty-three weeks tomorrow."

"Wow! We've only been here for six months. You must have been the first of the recruits to get pregnant. Obviously it didn't take you much time to find a suitable partner."

"Well Janet, the way it was explained to me, the gene enrichment program demanded expediency. I was just trying to do my part."

Fully aware that Kristyn possessed youthful and, at least for the moment, innocent ears with regard to the process of human reproduction, Janet spoke carefully. She said, "Indeed. I hope your enthusiasm for the project was pleasurable."

Natiya's cheeks, normally porcelain in color, showed a hint of blush as she replied, "Well Janet, it had been a long time since my enthusiasm, as you put it, was put to the test, but yes, it was pleasurable enough."

Nodding silently, Janet smiled at her distant memory of how a consensual first encounter could be accompanied by simultaneous exhilaration and nervousness. Then in desperate need of a solitary walk on the beach, Janet excused herself and added, "I'll catch up with the two of you later."

Two hours later, after contemplating how to best cope with the symptoms she was now beginning to experience, Janet returned to seek out Dr. Halley. She needed to converse with him about what had transpired with Ross, and her concern over the prospect that she might eventually face a similar challenge. That meeting would need to wait a few minutes however, as the doctor was just completing an examination of Janet's good friend Tori when she arrived.

As Tori exited the examination room with a smile, Janet said, "Good morning Tori. You look happy."

"I am. Dr. Halley says everything is fine."

"That's good news. How far along are you now, about eighteen weeks?"

The younger woman rubbed her pregnant belly in much the same way that Natiya had done, and then said, "Actually it's nineteen."

For Janet, Tori had become just one more of the many walking reminders of a time, and a condition, that she would never again experience. Although it was still physically possible at her current age of forty-three to become pregnant, Janet had no desire to carry a fourth child. The sight of several pregnant women within her population center was actually a positive sign that the gene enrichment program had moved into the fourth phase. Reports from the other fifteen such communities had also revealed an increase in pregnancies, so Janet felt justifiably pleased at the progress of the program. In spite of that feeling, it was difficult to see Tori as one of those in that condition. Although initially thrilled to learn that her good friend was expecting, Janet became less enthused when she discovered that the father of the child was Colt.

Once Tori had moved far enough away so that Janet felt safe in doing so, she dropped the façade that everything in her world was perfect. Then with justifiable concern in her tone, Janet looked at Dr. Halley and said, "If you haven't already heard, there has been a new development with Ross."

"Really, has he regained consciousness?"

"Yes he has, but it was how he regained consciousness that was alarming."

"Why? What happened?"

For twenty minutes Janet explained every detail of the adventure that had transpired in Ross's mind during the early morning hours. Then she asked, "Have you, or any of the other scientists, made any progress on a possible cure?"

Shaking his head negatively, Dr. Halley replied, "No. We haven't been able to isolate exactly what the virus is or how Ross contracted it in the first place, so developing a way to combat it is virtually impossible."

Janet slumped visibly, and then dejectedly asked, "How much longer do you think Ross has?"

Knowing that the depth of the question went beyond her concern for Ross, he replied, "I'm sorry Janet, but I just can't answer that with any level of certainty."

"That's what I was afraid of."

"How are your symptoms?"

"Well, they're not too bad yet. Every now and then I do experience some uncontrollable coughing or a slight fever, but not to the level that Ross goes through. I'm more concerned with what will happen to me in the future."

"I know that you are Janet, and because you're the most advanced case other than Ross, I'm concerned about you too. Knowing how quickly the virus takes full control of your body may help us determine a timeline for other cases, so you must be completely honest with me about what you experience."

After covering her face with trembling hands for a moment, she asked, "Is there any hope of containing the virus?"

"I'm afraid not, and we have received communications from the fifteen other population centers that several adults are beginning to experience some of the early symptoms."

"Do they suspect that they are infected with the virus?"

"No, and it's probably best that we keep it that way."

"I agree, but more importantly, Ross can't know about the virus either."

"Why not, he must be aware that you are ill."

"Yes he is aware, and he has seen a few symptoms with Gabriela and Aurora as well. Fortunately, he thinks we all have a cold based on our continued close contact with him."

"Well Janet, there is a measure of truth to his belief. After all, Ross is considered to be patient zero."

"Doctor, you and I, and the scientific team working on a cure know that to be true, but Ross doesn't need to know."

"Can't we at least tell him that we have no idea how to treat, let alone cure, his ailment?"

"No Doctor. Ross is a smart enough man to connect his illness with mine and everybody else's, so his heart and spirit would be broken by such knowledge. Imagine how you would feel if you learned that while once again attempting to save a percentage of the human species from possible extinction, you instead became the one most responsible for spreading a virus that could wipe it out!"

CHAPTER SEVEN

FALLEN OAK

Gabriela drew back the curtains, and the sunlight of the cloudless morning poured without obstruction into the room. While gazing out the window, she suddenly heard a loud thud from behind her. Turning to investigate, she noticed that Ross had fallen to the floor and was lying motionless. With fearful hesitation, Gabriela loudly asked, "Ross, are you alright?"

There was no response, so Gabriela repeated her question, and then she asked a third time before moving closer. Dropping to her knees at her husband's side, she attempted to awaken Ross by gently shaking his limp body. After checking his wrist for a pulse that no longer existed, Gabriela moved closer to his drawn face in order to determine if there was any sign of breathing. The results of each test, followed by feeling his chest for a heartbeat, had proven the awful, yet in some measure, merciful truth. Ross, her giant oak of a man, had just died.

Gabriela's initial reaction was to immediately inform someone, but then she realized that word of Ross's death would spread quickly enough on its own. She knew that one of the many daily visitors would eventually arrive to disrupt them, and in so doing, forever alter her life. Never again would she be able to spend a quiet peaceful moment alone with Ross. With that knowledge, Gabriela decided to lay next to Ross on the floor with her head resting on his shoulder for as long as time would permit. It was her turn to protect him from harm.

As if somehow aware of his coming fate, Ross had spent much of the three days since his last and most intense hallucination episode preparing his family and those closest to him for this inevitable moment. Although the anticipation of his death was a sad reality for all who knew him, Ross felt no personal regret. He had lived a long and productive life, while maintaining a steadfast belief in doing whatever he could to serve the betterment of mankind. His many actions throughout the years had more than proved his determination with regard to that belief system, and Ross had been blessed in several aspects of his life as a byproduct of those efforts. That included the most truly unforeseen chance for Ross to return to his birth world of Earth, as he was granted the opportunity to oversee one final act of humanitarian service. Unfortunately, the now obvious reality of his limited life span would prohibit Ross from ever witnessing the momentous fifth phase of the overall gene enrichment program. Reluctantly, Ross had accepted that he would never hold, or even receive knowledge of, a child born from the efforts of a brave recruit who had ventured with him from ₹-593-ॐπ-2-2.

Unaware, as most are, of the exact moment that his life would come to an end, Ross had been most fortunate that one of his lengthy pre-death discussions had been with young Hank. The two brothers, separated in age by roughly three quarters of an Earth century, had exchanged viewpoints on a wide range of subjects during a relaxing few hours on the beach just two days before Ross's death. Possessing an ability to absorb information like a sponge, Hank continued to develop that innate skill at every opportunity that presented itself. Just as he had done with Megan Crenshaw and every other adult influence in his life, Hank soaked up all the wisdom that Ross had to offer. Ross was proud of how his half-brother had developed intellectually at such a young age, and he was not alone in that assessment. Closing out their educational exchange by voicing his opinion to Hank, Ross had said, "You are a special young man, and it has been my honor to watch you grow into such an intelligent and caring person. Comparing you to my level of development at the same age, I believe that greatness awaits you."

Roughly twenty minutes after lying down beside her husband's dead body, Gabriela's less than bold prediction came to fruition. While hearing a gentle knocking on the door to their dwelling, she knew that the time of tranquility with Ross was gone forever. After kissing him gently on the cheek, she asked, "Who is it?"

"It's Aurora. Can I come in?"

"Yes Aurora. Please do."

Swinging the door open, Aurora began her customary greeting of, "Good morning..." Before she could say another word, Gabriela cut her off by responding, "Not for me it isn't. Ross is dead."

Only then did Aurora notice that her father and step mother were flat on the floor, and the tears that were clearly visible upon Gabriela's exposed cheek. For a brief moment she placed an open hand over her mouth, and then with a burst of unfiltered emotion exclaimed, "That can't be!"

Through her now muffled sobs and labored breathing, Gabriela replied, "I'm afraid it's true."

Although realizing that her obvious questions could, and most probably should, wait for another time, Aurora was unable to do so. She asked, "How, and when, did it happen?"

"It happened maybe half an hour ago. Everything was fine, and then he just fell over with a mighty thud!"

Now struggling to fight back her own onrush of grieving tears, Aurora moved to Gabriela's side, knelt down, and then reached out to rub her shoulder. Having now lost the battle with her emotions, through welling tears and trembling voice she uttered, "I'm so sorry Gabriela. Dad loved you very much, and you gave him the strength he needed to carry on the fight for humanity."

Turning her head away from Ross, Gabriela realized that she was not the only one in need of comfort. In spite of being Ross's wife for roughly eight years of Earth time, Gabriela understood that, as her father, Aurora had idolized Ross for her entire life. With that in mind she rose to a seated position next to Aurora and replied, "Your father was a wonderful man, and he never expressed any regrets at having used up so much of his fading strength attempting to help others."

Her words had fully opened the floodgates for both of them, as they began an embrace of uncontrollable crying. A few minutes later, after each woman had regained a measure of composure, they moved to the chairs at the table in the center of the room. Then Aurora said, "I think we should send word to Dr. Halley and Janet that they should come immediately."

Agreeing with the suggestion, Gabriela replied, "I'll be alright here for a few minutes. Why don't you do what you can to locate them?"

Stepping outside, Aurora hailed the closest citizen. Then she asked the young lady to locate Janet and Dr. Halley, and notify them that Ross had just passed away. Although shocked by the news, the woman was efficient with her given task. Within ten minutes Colt and Janet rushed through the door, and no more than five minutes later Dr. Halley arrived. In the first instance, the newcomers were welcomed by the sight of Ross motionless on the floor, and the silhouette of Gabriela and Aurora silently gazing out the sunlit window. Colt knelt at the body of his old friend and boss, while Janet joined the ladies by the window. As one aspect of a group effort, she could now provide, and receive, some much needed comfort.

Dr. Halley, while short of breath, burst through the door and asked, "Does anyone know how it happened?"

Gabriela was unable to respond, so Aurora said, "Ross just suddenly collapsed right where he is."

A few minutes later, after a preliminary examination of the body had been completed, Dr. Halley announced, "I can confirm that Ross died less than an hour ago. I can't tell you the exact cause at this time, but it appears to have been very quick and painless."

Janet snapped her head around in the direction of Dr. Halley. She, along with anyone else paying moderately close attention to Ross's affliction, knew that his death had been anything but quick and pain-less. Then realizing that the doctor was just doing his best to lessen the harsh reality of the present moment, Janet stood silently while resisting an overwhelming urge to correct his assessment.

ς

CHAPTER EIGHT

TEMPERED DISCLOSURE

Within the medical facility, the conversation topic that Janet and Dr. Halley shared with Gabriela was most certainly delicate in nature, but it was also necessary. In order to solicit Gabriela's help, they had jointly decided that she deserved to know everything. After vowing, at least in the short term, to remain silent about the content of the upcoming briefing, Gabriela listened intently to all that was conveyed. Although Janet and Dr. Halley, along with those of the dedicated scientific team working on the problem, were still perplexed as to the true origin and complexity of the virus, they openly shared what was known with her. Once she realized how the process might assist with the greater good, and knowing Ross had based many of his decisions on that same belief system, Gabriela reluctantly agreed. With a stern look in her eye, Gabriela then said, "I hope you understand my initial hesitation, and please maintain the appropriate level of respect for Ross while doing so, but I agree that a complete autopsy of his body is in order. Like you, I need to know exactly what caused his death."

Janet replied, "Thank you Gabriela. I promise you that neither of us has any intention of disrespecting him, so we will put forth our best effort."

Nodding positively, Gabriela replied, "Thank you. Now will you please allow me one final private moment with Ross before you begin? After that, he's in your hands."

After working for nearly eight hours with Dr. Halley on the autopsy and the recording of their findings, Janet needed a break. What they had discovered unfortunately proved that Ross must have suffered through a horrific final moment of life.

Early in the autopsy process, the chest cavity was cut open to reveal that their task would be more challenging than was originally believed. Gasping with disbelief, Dr. Halley said, "It looks as if both of the lungs suddenly exploded!"

With a look of concern from her seated position next to the computer, Janet impulsively placed a hand on her own chest and said, "Did you say exploded?"

Turning his gaze toward who might be the next patient to face a similar fate, he replied, "I'm afraid so."

Unfortunately the knowledge of what had ultimately killed Ross was of little comfort to them, as there was still the unanswered question of why the virus had created such a violent reaction. Long before ceasing their research efforts for the day, both Janet and Dr. Halley agreed that the newfound information should remain a secret. Although it was true that Gabriela could be trusted to remain silent about the virus and the global implication of its seemingly uncontrollable spread, it would serve no purpose for her to know that Ross had briefly endured such intense pain just prior to his death.

Emerging from Dr. Halley's medical facility, Janet began her search for Colt and Hank. She and Colt had only the briefest opportunity to speak with Hank about Ross's death earlier that day, and Janet felt that the conversation had been incomplete. Although Colt had remained available to provide support and field any questions that their son might have, the immediate need for the autopsy had pulled Janet away. That absence was now rectified, as the three of them sat peacefully on the beach while gazing up at the stars.

As Hank let a handful of sand slip through his fingers, Janet asked, "Did you have a chance to say goodbye to Ross?"

A few seconds later, Hank replied, "Although I didn't see him this morning before he died, yes I did. We talked for a few hours in almost this very spot just two days ago."

"You did? Well that's nice."

Placing an arm around his son, Colt then asked, "Is that when he gave you his fishing pole and the necklace?"

Drying the tears that had welled up in his eyes, Hank answered, "He gave me the necklace here at the beach, but the fishing pole was after we walked back to his dwelling."

"I see. Well what did you two talk about?"

Now turning toward his father, he said, "As usual we talked about several different topics, but it was what Ross said just before we walked back that I will vow never to forget."

"And what was that?"

"Ross told me that he believed greatness awaits me."

Janet was intrigued by her sons claim, and said, "That was nice of Ross to say that. Did he explain why?"

Before Hank could reply, Colt offered up verification of the claim. He added, "Ross and I had a lengthy conversation as well a few days ago, and he also informed me that he believed greatness awaited Hank."

Looking toward her husband with a smile, Janet said, "That's wonderful that Ross said that about Hank to both of you, but my question remains unanswered. Although I agree with his assessment, can you please tell me why Ross had such a belief?"

Colt then proudly replied, "Well let's see now. To begin with, Ross claimed that Hank had an ability to understand and absorb most of what people were attempting to teach him. Then he stated that Hank also knew how to process the information provided, and logically formulate a plan to solve whatever problems were presented. Next he spoke about how Hank had already developed a trust in his gut instinct to recognize, listen to, and respect the opinions of others that knew more about the discussion topic at hand. He mentioned communication skills, and that Hank used them effectively with people of most ages. Ross also made it clear that each of those traits were important aspects for leadership. Finally, he claimed that the most important reason for Hank's future greatness was the two of us. Ross said that Hank had a built-in advantage over him because we have, and always will, support Hanks ambitions every step of the way."

Shaken by the knowledge that the virus could prevent the final portion of that statement from becoming a reality, Janet turned her attention to Hank. Then with a tear in her eye she said, "It was very nice that Ross said all those things about your abilities, and he was correct. Your father and I will always encourage you to remain ambitious."

"I agree that it was nice of him mom, but when Ross first talked to me about my advantage I didn't fully understand. Then he pointed out that although we had a common mother, the conditions of our upbringing were different. Your abduction when he and Jessica were children, which was presented to them and everybody else as your death, created a tremendous void in their lives. Then everything about that time in his childhood became clear to me when he added an opinion of their father. Ross said dad was a more caring, dependable, and supportive man than his father Robert ever was."

Janet was saddened by the fact that her abduction had not only left an understandable void in the life of her first two children, but that the event had also changed the demeanor and character of the man she met at Roswell who had fathered them. Clasping Hank's hand she then said, "It was unfortunate for everyone involved that I wasn't around for Ross and Jessica, but something positive came out of it. Colt and I would never have been your parents if I hadn't been abducted."

"I know that mom, and so did Ross. He just wanted me to be aware that I had an advantage by having both of you around all the time."

Sensing that, for Janet's sake, the subject needed to be changed, Colt looked to the stars and asked, "Hey Hank, I know it's located somewhere in the constellation of Orion, but do you remember which star our old home is orbiting around?"

Without hesitation Hank pointed skyward and replied, "Of course I do dad, I promised Ross that I would never forget. You see the three stars running down from the three that form Orion's Belt? Those form the great hunter's sword, and our moon is in orbit around the faint star just to the right of the tip."

Janet looked to the stars to locate their former world, and then after a silent moment of contemplation said, "I hope many of Ross's life lessons stick with you Hank, but you should also know that there is much more to leadership than a list of positive skills and traits that he correctly believed you possess. He understood, and never forgot, that his leadership could not have been obtained without the help of others. Each of us also know that Ross was a humble man, and that may be the most important trait that any leader of people should possess. He has demonstrated that humility several times with his ability to publicly admit, unlike some other leaders of his time on Earth, when he had made an incorrect decision."

"You mean like back on our former home moon when Ross and I traveled into unexplored territory without having anyone else with us?"

"Well, yes. That's an excellent example. If I remember correctly, Ross fell on that little adventure and hurt himself."

"Yes he did. Ross lost his footing, and got a whole bunch of scrapes and cuts all over his body when he tumbled down that hill through the thorny bushes. Then he landed face first into a puddle of clear liquid. Ross told me that it tasted awful, and felt like some kind of thick syrup."

Roughly thirty-six hours after their discussion on the beach, Janet, Colt, and Hank joined Aurora and Tikal in a unified effort to comfort Gabriela. The somber family gathering took place on a small rise a few hundred yards from the beach, and also included friends such as Natiya, Kristyn, Tori, Dr. Halley and others who wished to pay their respects. Although the event lacked the extreme level of pomp associated with similar ones held centuries before in honor of his predecessors, the service did possess the respectful dignity befitting a former President of the United States.

The journey that had enabled Ross to view many regions of Earth through both personal visitations and from the sky above, then his leading of the human pilgrimage to a new world in a solar system far beyond where mankind had previously thought to venture, and the eventual return to his birth world, had ended very close to where it all began. In accordance with his final wishes, Ross had been put to rest in ground that, for the briefest moment in Earth's history, was known as Texas. Fulfilling a promise that she had made to Ross during her grandfather Robert's funeral when she was only eight years old, Aurora faithfully carried out her given task. Now decades later by her internal body clock, and more than twenty-six centuries of elapsed Earth time, Aurora wrapped Ross in a cloak of honor. The American flag that had once been draped over the casket for the military funeral of her great-grandfather Hank, and then presented to Ross for safe-keeping long before her birth, now engulfed Ross as he was lowered into his grave.

Shortly after the conclusion of the service, with Gabriela safely steadied by the strength of Colt's arm, Janet sought out Dr. Halley. Then speaking softly so that no one else could hear, she said, "Unfortunately it will be impossible for us to obtain a sample of the substance that was responsible, but I believe I know when Ross became infected with the virus and how it entered his system."

$$\text{♪}$$

CHAPTER NINE

A BLAST FROM THE PAST

Throughout the initial few weeks following the funeral for Ross, Colt had been keeping a diligent watch on the actions of Hank. There could be no denial that his young son was currently in a deep funk of depression, and that mindset was justifiable. Colt was also honest with himself, as he understood that he shared similar feelings of grief. After all, they, along with many others both within the family and on the peripheral, had just lost a person of tremendous significance within their life's journey.

Knowing that something needed to be done in order to help both Hank and himself emerge from the fog, Colt called upon an idea that he and Ross had discussed on occasion. Waiting for the opportune moment when he and his son would be alone, Colt then asked, "Hey Hank, you know those large vehicles that are used for transporting food to the citizens from the hydroponics facility?"

With head hung low while picking over his plate of fresh vegetables, Hank replied, "Sure dad. Those same vehicles also transport water and ice from the desalinization plant."

"That's right, and do you know how those vehicles are powered?"

"Sure. They use a large bank of collectors on the roof and side panels to harness solar power."

"Right again, and I was thinking that maybe you and I could try to build a similar vehicle."

"Similar?"

"Sure. We could start with the basic concept that those vehicles have, and then make a few modifications."

Colt knew instantly that his plan had created a spark of interest within his ever curious son, as Hank turned his gaze toward him and asked, "What kind of modifications?"

"Well, although the solar panels are a fantastic way to harness energy, the speed of the vehicles and nighttime use is limited by their bulk and the storage capacity of what energy has been collected."

"That's true, but can that be corrected?"

"Yes. I was thinking of constructing a smaller model of the vehicles for personal use, while also adding two alternative sources of power to the equation."

"Alternate power sources? Like what?"

"Well, wind power for one."

"Wind power?"

"Sure. You know there is usually a steady gentle breeze blowing throughout the region, so Ross and I began kicking around an idea a few months ago. We had remembered that during our former time on Earth, some people enjoyed their recreation time by playing around in the desert. Although many of them preferred the use of a two or four wheeled motorized vehicle for transportation, a few simply captured the wind so that it would push them across the arid landscape."

"Push them? That sounds cool, but how did they do it?"

"In most cases they built a triangular metal frame with three wheels underneath, and then raised a sail on a vertical mast to capture the wind and move them forward. When they wanted to stop, they just lowered the sail."

"What a great idea!"

"It sure was, but it wasn't a modern invention. The idea stemmed from many centuries before when people needed to harness the wind in order to cross the vast oceans in boats. That concept provided a free and clean energy source for anyone to use, and it eventually morphed into very limited use on land and in the sky above. Unfortunately, that alternative method to move about never really caught on with the masses."

"What did they do when there was no wind?"

"That was the main problem, because with no wind, the three wheeled desert vehicles couldn't go anywhere without motorized assistance. Ross and I hoped to alleviate the issues associated with those vehicles, and the problems associated with the ones used here for transporting food, water, and ice. By combining the ancient use of wind with the more modern technology of solar power, I think that you and I could do that."

"That sounds like a good idea, but you also mentioned something about a second alternative power source?"

"You have probably never heard of the device known as a bicycle before, as I haven't seen one around here and we didn't have any on your birth moon either. Nevertheless, pedal power would be a fantastic addition to our vehicle."

"Pedal power, what is that?"

Using the best visual technique that he could muster from a seated position, Colt explained how a bicycle worked and how such a device had been an excellent means of healthy transport for the masses within certain societies around the globe. Then he said, "If you and I could figure out a plausible way to apply a sail to our smaller solar vehicle, and fit each seat with a set of pedals underneath, then we would have a vehicle with three sources of power for use anytime of the day or night."

"That sounds really cool. When can we get started?"

"We can start working on it today if you want to. After we finish eating, why don't we put some thoughts down on paper and speak with some engineers in the manufacturing plant. They could probably help us build or locate most of the parts and material that we will need."

From that moment, Colt and Hank's thoughts became consumed by their new project. When Janet returned from yet another long day of research at the medical facility, she found her son and husband looking over drawings and a large stack of odds and ends. She didn't really care to know what they were involved with at the present moment, but it came as a welcome sight. Their body language and boyish grins were evidence that the pile of debris had provided a necessary distraction, and had definitely altered their recent state of mind.

That evening, Janet sat silently while waiting for an explanation of their intent. When none was offered, curiosity eventually overpowered her and she inquired, "Hank, what are you and your father doing with that stack of odds and ends?"

"It's a project that could help the community."

"Really, can you tell me what it is?"

"Not right now mom, but after we finish building it, I'll tell you all about it."

Glancing at her husband, Janet could plainly see Colt's wry smile. That was his subtle way of protecting a trust, so she looked back at Hank, and replied, "All right then. The two of you can have your little secret for now."

Early the next morning, construction began in earnest. Colt and Hank put together the elongated triangular mainframe, and positioned the three large wheels beneath the pointed extremities for added stability. The next step was to construct the seating area, which was designed to have a singular seat for the driver placed in the narrower portion of the vehicle directly in front of the stump for the hinged mast. Two seats in a single file would then be positioned on each side of where the mast would lay flat when not in use. Each seat had ample legroom, with a set of bicycle style pedals placed in front of them.

Turning their attention to the undercarriage, Colt took the lead role in the assembly effort. Beyond what had been needed for the mainframe, the manufacturing plant had been most helpful by providing several pieces of gear fabricated to Colt's specifications. Having also delivered their creations the previous afternoon, those same engineers who performed the work had now returned to see how Colt and Hank intended to use them. Watching with a keen eye as assembly began, they, along with Hank, asked several questions throughout the process. Hank's interest was further peaked when Colt said, "Ross told me once about how he used pedals, sprockets, and connecting chains just like these to power his model of Earth's solar system for a school project when he was ten years old."

That thought burned into Hank's memory, as he replied, "Ross told me about that model too, but he never mentioned how it had been powered."

Once work on the undercarriage had been completed to Colt's liking, the next step in the process could commence. The lightweight metal boom housing the sail became part of the mast structure by slipping the attached metal ring over the stump. Then the mast was moved into position between the two long protruding flanges of the stump, and a large sturdy pin was driven through the four precisely aligned holes near the base. Colt then demonstrated to the growing and inquisitive crowd of how easy it would be to raise the mast. Turning to Hank, he said, "Could you please hoist the mast into a vertical position, and then push the mast pin through the four aligned holes at the top end of the flanges."

Without hesitation Hank jumped up and began the process. After quickly completing the task, he turned to his father and said, "That was easy, the mast is really light."

"That's why I had you lift it Hank. Now all these people know that any of them would be capable of hoisting the mast into position if the need arose."

"Should I put a locking pin through the hole at the end of the mast pin like we did with the larger hinge pin?"

Moving to a position upon the mainframe next to the driver's seat, Colt replied, "No thanks Hank." Then turning to the engineers and others who had gathered, he pointed to the mast while adding in a louder voice, "Unlike the locking pin at the end of the hinge pin that is permanent, this locking pin is only for use when the mast is vertical. At such a time, it is imperative that the locking pin be inserted through the mast pin." After receiving verifying nods of understanding from all those present, Colt returned his gaze toward his son. With a softer tone, he then said, "Hank, would you please remove the mast pin and lower the mast back to a horizontal position."

After once again easily completing the assigned task, Hank revealed his eagerness by asking, "What's next dad?"

"I think before we go any further with the construction, we should test out the bicycle aspect. How do you feel about taking this thing for a ride?"

"That would be cool, but do we need any help?"

"You mean with the pedaling? No we don't, because the lightweight design of the vehicle should enable a single person to pedal it forward. If you want to, you can ask the engineers if any of them want to go for a ride."

A short time later Tori, while looking out her window, noticed a strange sight. Five people were moving past on some weird contraption, and the man at the front was Colt. Before she could emerge from her dwelling to get a closer look they had turned the corner, so she asked a passerby, "Excuse me, did you see that weird thing that just came through here?"

The old woman was suffering through a rather harsh coughing spell, but during a temporary respite, did manage to reply, "Yes I did, but I have no idea what it was."

Tori's impulse to locate and identify the bizarre object was delayed, as she rushed back inside for some water to ease the poor woman's suffering. While tending to her needs, they were both suddenly surprised when Colt said, "Hello Tori, how are you doing today?"

Apparently Colt and his party had routed themselves so as to return to Tori's dwelling, and now she spun around to find that their apparatus had come to rest within twenty feet of her position. Instinctively placing a hand on her pregnant belly, Tori smiled and replied, "I'm fine Colt. How are you?"

"Great thanks. With the help of some engineers from the manufacturing plant, Hank and I started building something that could be beneficial to the community."

"Well that's good to hear, but what is it?"

"It's an alternative mode of transportation that anyone can use, but we haven't finished building it yet. Actually, I was hoping that you could help us with a design problem?"

"Perhaps, but first tell me what the problem is."

"Well, one aspect of this vehicle will be solar power, and a portion of the collector panels will be placed at an angle along each length of the mainframe. That will capture some energy, but we need a larger overhead surface area as well."

"So you need to speak with a solar engineer. That shouldn't be a problem. I'll need to check their schedules, but one of them could probably help you tomorrow."

"Thanks Tori. That would be great."

The following morning, a young woman approached Colt and Hank while they worked on the vehicle. With a smile she said, "Hello, I'm Kenna Hayden. Tori mentioned that you've encountered a design problem, how can I help?"

Colt turned and said, "You must be the solar engineer that she spoke of, and thanks for the offer to help Ms. Hayden. What we need is a large collector panel above the seating area of the vehicle, but it can't be one solid piece."

"I understand, and please, call me Kenna. Now, can you tell me why the panel can't be one solid piece?"

Looking at Hank, he said, "Could you please show Kenna how the mast will work?"

After repositioning the mast to its upright position and locking it into place, Hank said, "Because we will need to raise or lower this depending on the wind conditions."

"Did you say the wind conditions?"

"Yes ma'am. Wind will be one source of our power."

Kenna nodded her head as she suddenly grasped their intended concept. Then looking back at Colt, she said, "I think I have an idea that could help."

"That's great. Tell me about it please."

Their subsequent discussion led to sketches, and then a trip to the manufacturing plant. Later that same day, Colt and Hank, with help from Kenna and others, were able to fit the final pieces of their vehicle into place. Supported by several vertical struts, the overhead solar array began at a point near the nose of the vehicle and then split into two sections just forward of the mast position. Never exceeding the width, but protruding beyond the back of the vehicle, the two slightly curved panels with a wide gap between them reminded Colt of the large folded wings of a bug.

With construction complete, Hank remained true to his word. That evening he informed Janet of everything that the vehicle was capable of, and the altered state of transportation that had been created in the process. Then he asked her, "So mom, when can we take you out for a ride?"

CHAPTER TEN

WIND IN THE HAIR

With Colt having assumed the drivers position, he, along with Janet and Hank, had peddled the prototype vehicle to the northern edge of the population center. With nothing but the semi-flat and windswept open spaces in front of them, Colt asked, "Hey Hank, are you ready to raise the sail for a trial run?"

"Sure dad, let's do it."

Janet, who had never experienced riding the wind in a boat or any other manner, showed a noticeable look of concern. Colt was quick to ease her apprehension by saying, "I promise you, it's completely safe. This new type of vehicle is in sharp contrast to what you and I remember from our time on old Earth. The focus is on simple technology that should have been developed more significantly back then, and I'm pleased that this modern society is more accepting of alternative concepts."

Nodding positively, Janet replied, "Alright, I trust you."

Within seconds after hearing those words, Hank raised the mast to vertical, locked it in place, and said, "All set here."

After a verifying nod, Colt pulled on the line that slid the boom up the mast above the level of the solar canopy. Once that was secure he pulled another line to unfurl a portion of the sail from within, and the vehicle began to move forward. A moment later he turned to notice that Janet and Hank were smiling, so he asked, "What do you think, should we go faster?"

Hank exclaimed, "Yes! Let's go as fast as we can!"

Obviously outnumbered, Janet realized that a negative response would be ignored, so she replied, "Sure, why not?"

Colt then unfurled more of the sail, and adjusted the angle of the boom to maximize the winds thrust. The difference in speed was immediate as the vehicle lurched forward, and soon after that, Hank joyously shouted out, "This is really cool."

Janet couldn't contain that she was also enjoying the ride, which was smoother than she had originally visualized, so she added, "I agree, this is fun."

As Colt tested the maneuverability and turning radius at various levels of sail deployment, Hank paid close attention to his father's technique. While soaking up knowledge about the safe operation of the vehicle, he also noticed that they must have slowly circled around back toward the population center. The lights of the community were now in full frontal view, so Hank said, "We aren't going back home yet are we?"

Before Colt could reply, Janet spoke up. While looking west through the darkness toward the last faint hint of sunlight cast upon the sets of orbital rings, she said, "I think that we should head back home. It's getting late, and we do have to pedal this thing again after dropping the sail."

Fully aware that Janet had been extremely patient with them during the recent days and weeks, and had exhibited graciousness while reluctantly admitting her enjoyment during the trial run, Colt concurred. He said, "I think that your mother is right Hank. It's time to go home."

The trials of the following night would be a different story however, as Colt stayed out until the first hint of daylight while providing numerous rides. Although each passenger understood the basics of solar power for vehicles and the everyday uses within their dwellings, the other power sources of the new vehicle were conceptually foreign. Colt took several groups of four out for a quick loop via their own pedal power, and then showcased the ease of handling and maneuverability for roughly an hour under sail. The first passengers consisted of Tori, Kenna, and two engineers from the manufacturing plant who had aided with construction. They each in their own way marveled at what they were all experiencing, and quickly realized the vast potential that wind power could offer to each of the population centers. At the completion of their tour, Tori approached Colt and exclaimed, "Thank you for enlightening us to this concept. It's fantastic!"

"You're welcome Tori. I'm glad that you enjoyed it."

"How did you come to know about such things?"

"Ross taught me everything that he knew about the principles of sailing on the water. According to him, it was just one aspect of the basic fundamentals that he learned while attending the Naval Academy."

"Well whatever the source of his knowledge, I'm glad that he shared it with you. I believe it's important that we pass this technology along to everyone, so I will begin contacting the other population centers first thing in the morning."

"I guess that proves that at least some of the ancient technology of Earth could be considered a benefit to those living within the present time."

"True, and beyond those beneficial uses, there was one aspect of the ride that was also quite liberating."

"Really, what was that?"

"It felt good to move as fast as we did, and experience the wind blowing through my hair."

ſ
Ź

CHAPTER ELEVEN

ALTERED STATES

Planet wide cooperation was once again exemplified, as Tori spent the entire next day within the communication center conferring with representative administrators and engineers from the other fifteen population centers. She spoke highly of the new transportation mode that Colt and Hank had not only envisioned, but with the help of local engineers, had also built and successfully tested. While using the computer to forward all of the notes, sketches, and design specifications associated with the prototype vehicle, Tori also informed her counterparts that construction on several more of the vehicles would begin in her community within the next few days. Armed with that information, and Tori's promise that Colt or Hank would be available for subsequent questions, each community felt they had the tools they needed to proceed with assembly.

Throughout the next few months, Tori would receive, and subsequently share with Colt, any news from the various population centers with regard to their current stages of vehicle development. Although a few communities had been passive with their interest in the concept, most had been quite eager to move forward with developing an altered state of the vehicle that would best suit their respective needs.

One example of such exuberance rose from the former Canadian province of British Columbia. Within the settlement just east of where Vancouver had been located, the alternative modes of transportation came as a welcome relief. While speaking with a team of their engineers via the communication center, Colt learned that although solar energy had been employed as a power source for centuries, it could not be counted upon for much of the year. The weather patterns in and around the mountainous region unfortunately caused cloud cover more often than not, so the use of solar powered vehicles had been abandoned. What limited solar energy that had been available and harnessed, had always been prioritized for the desalinization and hydroponics facilities. Beyond that, needs of the manufacturing plant or those within individual dwellings were met before anything else could even be considered. Consequently, those that remained of their ever dwindling population were some of the most physically fit citizens on the planet, as trudging up and down the often steep and heavily wooded terrain became the only way to perform their daily activities.

Colt's distant and somewhat fuzzy memory of the region was brought into sharper focus when an engineer said, "Your design concept developed from a combination of old Earth technologies will be an extremely beneficial addition to our community. Although we often lack consistent sunshine, wind is abundant throughout the region."

Colt quickly replied, "Thank you, and in spite of all the turmoil that this planet has endured through time, it sounds as if, at least in your region, that the atmospheric conditions have returned to the patterns of the era before the asteroid and moon impacts."

"You speak as if you know this area. Did you live near here before the apocalypse?"

"No, but I did visit once for an extended fishing trip."

"A fishing trip, was that common back then?"

"For avid fisherman it was. I remember that the city of Vancouver was very nice, and the surrounding countryside was beautiful with forested landscapes, rugged shorelines, and lots of fish in the ocean, lakes, and rivers."

"You have just described our region with incredible accuracy, so that is apparently another aspect that has returned to pre-apocalyptic times. Fishing remains a major aspect of our daily survival, and the introduction of wind aided craft will enhance our ability to meet the supply needs of our citizens. As to what remains of the abandoned city to our west, I was not aware that it was once known as Vancouver. Evidence of a few old structures in crumbled ruins can be seen along portions of the neighboring hillsides, but thick vegetation has overtaken most of them. There are records of how unsafe the ruins were as many former citizens were either killed or injured during various collapses, and those areas were subsequently declared off-limits. Other much taller structures still rise through the water of the bay, but I learned as a boy that all of them have been unoccupied for many centuries. During extremely windy days, we can sometimes see large waves pounding against those structures, and I wonder if another will fall over."

"Another one, does the evidence you spoke of mention any of the taller ones collapsing?"

"Yes it does, but I also witnessed one of them falling when I was a boy. My friends and I were dodging the big waves on a clear windy day when all of a sudden we heard a loud cracking noise. We looked over just in time to see that one of the structures was breaking apart not far above the surface. It crashed into the bay in basically one large piece, but it took us all a minute to realize that it also created a much larger wave that was coming towards us. We ran up the hill away from shore as fast as we could, and then turned to watch the wave come in. It caused minimal damage to our community, but not long after that day, the administrators decided to relocate our population center a little further to the east."

"That's amazing! You and your friends were in the right place at the precise moment within a twenty-six century timeframe to witness something like that happen."

"I suppose that's one way to look at it, but there must have been countless people around the planet throughout the centuries to witness a similar poignant example of Earth's past civilization disintegrating before their eyes."

The man had made an astute observation, and it sent a chill up Colt's spine. As a consequence, Colt suddenly became lost in the thought of how many global seaside communities, be they small hamlets or large mega cities, had been obliterated. The number was uncountable with any true level of accuracy, and it was a wonder that remnants of other coastal skyscrapers could still exist anywhere on the planet. If the nearly endless salvo of massive tsunamis created by the impacts of the apocalypse hadn't done them in, then the eventual dramatic rise in the ocean levels would have finished them off. What hadn't been permanently submerged had simply become sets of pillars surrounded by the relentless erosive power of water and surf. Given enough time, no tower of corporate arrogance from the early twenty-first century society could stand defiantly. They would all eventually crumble into the sea.

Colt's train of thought was interrupted when Tori began pushing on his shoulder while pointing to the communication console as the distant voice asked, "Colt, are you still there?"

"What? Oh, I'm sorry about that. I was just thinking about something else and I didn't hear what you said."

The engineer on the other end of the line replied, "No problem Colt. I was just saying that now, thanks to you, we have built a few small wind powered vessels for use in the water. They have tested well, and our intent is to use them for transporting our catch of fish from greater distances. As for the community, a few wheeled vehicles have been constructed to facilitate our distribution needs."

"That's wonderful news, but I hope you incorporated the bicycle aspect into your land vehicles as well. It sounds to me as if many members of your community are physically fit enough to employ pedal power into their routines."

"Indeed we have, and if Tori can spare you, I invite you to visit our community in the future. You can take a look at our altered state of your design, and perhaps you and I could do a little fishing while you're here."

"Thank you, that's a nice offer. I don't know if such a trip would be possible though, as people other than Tori would need to approve before I could even consider it."

Colt didn't know it at the time, but that conversation would be the first of many with engineers from around the planet. With Hank seated beside him for the majority of those conversations, they learned, among other things, that the two population centers located near what had formerly been Tokyo Japan and Hong Kong China had each latched onto the sailboat concept for fishing. Then using different designs, they had also developed a bicycle style vehicle for their respective needs.

In the North African settlement, on what little land mass remained of southern Egypt, solar energy had been plentiful for use as a power source. Although the extreme heat and dry air of the region created a detriment with regard to incorporating pedal power, the population did embrace the concept of adding sails to their solar vehicles.

Eventually, Colt and Hank learned that an example of their design had been developed in an altered state by each of the population centers. Throughout that process, they had also become celebrities within the eyes of the global engineering community. Janet found it humorous to observe her husband and son as they each navigated their way through the potential pitfalls of stardom. Hank, as one would expect of a boy his age, thought the additional attention was cool. That is, as long as the administrators and engineers didn't treat him like a boy of his age. As for Colt, he had been expertly trained to do so, and had then gladly spent much of his adult years standing as the protective shadow for a person in the limelight. With that in mind, Janet knew that Hank would be well taken care of by his father. The larger question, especially considering her very busy research schedule, was who would watch out for Colt. Janet had noticed that a young woman in local circles had developed an increasing interest in Colt, and because he was completely oblivious to that fact, it became necessary for Janet to monitor his level of vulnerability against her intended actions.

When the opportune moment presented itself, Janet approached the young solar engineer with a smile and said, "You're Kenna Hayden aren't you? I know we have seen each other once or twice throughout the past few months when you were helping with the development of the prototype vehicle. I have always thought of you as a pleasant young woman who must possess a high level of intelligence."

Surprised by the approach and candor of the woman whom she believed had always intentionally kept her distance from the project, Kenna replied, "Yes, we have. I recognize you Janet, and I appreciate the kind words."

"Good. I'm glad to know that you recognize me Kenna, and you're welcome. Now if I may, I have something important to discuss with you."

"Alright Janet, would you like to sit down?"

"No thanks, this will only take a minute. It's important that you fully understand I have nothing against you personally, but we cannot, and will not, become close friends."

Shocked by the quick reversal of Janet's initial warm approach, Kenna replied, "Well, I believe that would be most unfortunate for both of us. Is there a particular reason why you feel that way?"

"Yes there is Kenna. I'm already very good friends with one such person, and that makes our relationship more difficult than it needs to or used to be. I have always been aware that my husband would become a necessary participant in the gene enrichment program, but I don't, other than casually, have a desire to know the various women who have selected him for that purpose."

CHAPTER TWELVE

ONE REVOLUTION

Working in conjunction with Tori at the communication center, Aurora sent a message out to each recruit living in the various population centers around the globe. In the event that other individuals hadn't kept a record of such matters, Aurora wanted it known that this day marked the completion of one full Earth year since their arrival from ₹-593-३ए-2-2.

After concluding her transmission, Aurora slipped into several moments of quiet self-reflection. Having been tasked by Ross with the meticulous and vital records associated with the gene enrichment program, Aurora was happy that phase five had begun to bear fruit. The birth of babies due to the efforts of several recruits had been reported from around the globe during the past two months, and more women in each of the population centers were expected to add to that list shortly.

Natiya held the distinction among all of the recruits as being the first to deliver when she provided Kristyn with a baby sister, and the Peruvian runner whom Ross had suggested as the final member of the local group was in the late stages of pregnancy. The adult male recruits of the group, Colt and Tikal, had also done their part. A woman who chose Tikal to be the father of her child was due in less than a month, while another was now in her second trimester. Tori had not been far behind Natiya when she gave birth to Colt's daughter, and there had been recent confirmation that Kenna now carried his child.

While mentally reliving several events beyond the births which had transpired throughout the year, Aurora also paid respectful homage to the deaths and what had been the root cause for the majority of them. One such memory, the death of Ross, was more vivid than any other. She believed, from a purely personal and selfish angle, that Ross's death and the events surrounding it had been the low point of the year. Fortunately for Aurora, she was also cognizant of the fact that her feelings were not necessarily shared by the majority of the remaining human population of Earth. Although Ross had intended well with the implementation of the gene enrichment program, he had unknowingly unleashed an epidemic that was spreading throughout the sixteen population centers of the planet. There had been several dozen recent deaths, and unfortunately, each of the respective autopsies revealed the same exploded lungs that Ross had endured.

Returning to the present, Aurora just couldn't shake the feeling that there must be something more to each of the deaths than was originally believed. While once again mentally reviewing several of the cases, she suddenly realized that a hidden pattern might exist. Turning to Tori, she said, "Will you excuse me for a few moments? I must go check something in my records. If my belief is correct, then we need to speak with Janet and Dr. Halley immediately."

While cradling her sleeping child that was only days old, Tori replied, "Sure Aurora, no problem. But you make it sound so serious though, is there anything that I can do to help?"

"Not at the moment, but I may take you up on the offer when I return."

After scanning through her meticulous notes of births, deaths, and other events of significance for more than an hour, Aurora returned with a large notebook under her arm.

When she came through the door, Tori asked, "Well, did you find whatever it was that you were looking for?"

"I did indeed. Now will you please come with me? I must share this information with Janet and Dr. Halley."

"Of course I will, but can you at least tell me what you discovered before we go?"

"You'll know soon enough. Now come on, let's go."

The two women sped off toward the medical research labs with as much haste as could be managed while carrying an infant. Once there, they located Janet and Dr. Halley.

Turning toward the unexpected guests, Dr. Halley said, "Well hello ladies. Can I help you with something?"

Aurora then blurted out, "I have some information with regard to the virus that I believe is important!"

"Really, well what is it?"

"We have all been so busy looking at Ross as the source of the problem, that we couldn't see it."

"See what exactly?"

"If we could just look beyond the role of blame for Ross, and view the problem from a clinical angle, it's easy to see that his, and each of the other deaths, has been informative."

Janet intervened, "What are you getting at Aurora?"

"I believe that the mysterious virus strikes, and then advances within each host body, based on a level of prejudice."

"Interesting theory, could you explain it please?"

"Well, up to this point only adults have died. I have checked over my records thoroughly, and each person to have died was a minimum of sixty years old. Although there has been an ever increasing amount of adults under that age exhibiting the early symptoms, none of them have died yet. Additionally, there has been no report of infection within any of the children or newborns."

Dr. Halley responded first, "That's very interesting. Are you sure that your data is correct?"

"Yes I am Dr. Halley, without a doubt. Unless of course there was some incorrect information forwarded to me."

Having experienced the level of precision with regard to Aurora's documentation for several years, Janet announced, "I can vouch for her accuracy on such matters Dr. Halley. If Aurora claims there is a pattern in the data, then there is."

"Alright Janet, that's good enough for me. Now in order for us to proceed with this, we should first confirm that Aurora was indeed given correct information about those who have, or have not, become infected. Once that has been determined, then we can dig deeper into the data and see if it reveals any other patterns."

Aurora nodded, turned toward Tori, and asked, "Can you help me send out another message? I need to contact each of your counterparts in the other population centers."

"Sure, that's not a problem."

"Thank you. The sooner we can begin the research on my theory, the better it may be for everyone."

Throughout the next few days, the two women tended to their mission. They spoke with administrators and anyone else who might assist with validating Aurora's hypothesis. As records of those either killed by, or infected with, the deadly virus were further scrutinized, the reality of her claim became apparent.

Aurora remembered Janet saying that from the earliest days of attempting to combat the virus, the common belief was that Ross had been the initial carrier. Of that there could be no doubt. Additionally, there had been an early theory by some that the virus was spread via bodily fluids. Gabriela's intimacy with Ross, and her subsequent illness, had suggested that might be accurate, but it was the only real evidence to support such a belief. With no such personal contact, Janet, among the many others living both near and far to Ross's location, had provided proof that the virus was spread differently. Consequently, the bodily fluid thought process was quickly dismissed. Much like various strains of viruses during the time of old Earth, it was determined that this lethal bug was an airborne version.

Aside from being identified as patient zero, Ross also held the dubious distinction of having been the oldest to have died from it. Others who had met with the same sad fate during subsequent weeks and months varied in ages, but those victims created another interesting pattern. Aurora determined that as the age of each respective victim had decreased, the duration of time from the moment of their initial infection, on through the various symptom phases, and then to their eventual death, had increased.

Up to the moment of that enlightenment, Janet had been the most interesting and perplexing case due to how long she had survived since her exposure to the virus. Although it was unknown to her at the time, Janet's close proximity to Ross since the day he had contracted the virus weeks before leaving ₹-593-ℨπ-2-2 had placed her in jeopardy. The concentrated exposure to Ross had continued for the entire eight month duration of his illness, but her symptoms were much less pronounced. Now the age pattern for the dead that Aurora had stumbled upon helped to solve the question of why Janet had not only lived through such extreme exposure, but why she had also survived an additional six months.

Using the newly established template created by the respective ages of both Ross and Janet, those scientists working on the problem could now estimate, with reasonable accuracy, the life expectancy of a patient that had become infected. Additionally, Aurora's discoveries had also solved the puzzle of why every other person, with the exception of Gabriela, who returned to Earth with Ross was still alive. To that end, Aurora, now the most senior member of the remaining ninety-eight, pondered why her husband Tikal hadn't shown the slightest sign of infection. Although clearly exhibiting her own symptoms, she remained grateful that Tikal had somehow been spared up to this point. Then what suddenly occurred to her was that at no prior time had she bothered to question why.

For Aurora, the topic instantly became a question that demanded her attention. She inspected her notes closely with regard to those on the manifest, and once again an interesting pattern emerged from the data. Then bursting into the medical labs, Aurora looked at Janet and Dr. Halley, and exclaimed, "I have just discovered some additional information from the data that could be significant!"

As if in chorus, they responded, "What is it?"

"It's so obvious. I'm upset with myself because I didn't notice it before now."

Janet took the lead, and asked, "Notice what exactly?"

"Well, it's about the Mayan contingent that came with us from ₹-593-ʒπ-2-2."

"Fine, now please get to the point Aurora. What about the Mayan's is so important?"

"Regardless of their respective ages, up to and including Tikal, none of the twenty-one Mayans anywhere on the planet have shown any symptoms of becoming infected."

"None of them, are you sure?"

"Yes I am. We could easily have the respective medical personnel at each population center run blood tests to verify my findings, but if none of the Mayans come back as positive, then they may somehow be immune to the global virus."

CHAPTER THIRTEEN
IN QUEST OF BLOOD

Aurora's thesis was proven to be correct within the coming weeks, as each of the twenty-one Mayan recruits, including Tikal, had tested negative for the virus. What had actually proved to be more difficult than the testing itself was the task of locating a few members of the collective. Aurora's notes had been the primary and accurate source as to which population center that each recruit had been sent to, and in every community but one, they were located and tested with relative ease. The single problem area within that search was in the former South American continent.

Although the site located between the former Brazilian mega cities of Rio de Janeiro and Sao Paulo had been quick and easy, the community administrators along the west coast had less accountability as to the whereabouts of their citizens. That circumstance was magnified in two ways. First, the community where La Calera had once stood northwest of Santiago Chile was the third largest population center on the planet. Second, the group selected for that location was one of only five that contained two Mayan recruits. An organized hunt for each of them would begin immediately, but the local consensus was that they had separately headed into the nearby mountains.

When Tori delivered the news to Aurora, she replied, "Well that may prove to be quite a challenge, and please ask that the quest not be treated as a hunt. One of the many things that Gabriela taught me about the Mayan culture before she died was that they don't take kindly to being hunted."

"I understand, but wouldn't that increase the time it takes to locate each of them."

"Yes it may, but we need to expand the blood testing for the virus to every citizen within each of the population centers eventually. I know that we had hoped to test each of the Mayans first, but in La Calera, they will just begin the all-encompassing process before that can be done. Believe me Tori, the medical personnel within each community that are responsible for the testing will be busy for several days. Besides that, I don't believe that either of the two Mayans is actually hiding from anyone. They should be relatively easy to locate, and will be far less defensive, especially the male, if they learn that the testing is being done to all of the citizens. If however, they feel singled out, they may run for the hills. Each will undoubtedly need to access whatever the community has to offer at some point, and when they do, it's important that they see, or at least hear of, others being tested."

"Did Gabriela teach you all of that?"

"She taught me most of it, but being married to Tikal has helped shape my thinking as well."

By the time Aurora's prediction came to fruition, each test from the other nineteen Mayans had come back negative. The missing female, now pregnant with her second child, did emerge with her infant from a quiet retreat a few days after the search for her had begun. She complied, as many of her friends had already done, with the blood testing procedure for herself and the baby. It was unfortunate that a tremendous amount of time and resources needed to be applied during the search for the young male, but as finding and testing him was imperative, the quest for his blood would continue.

As he had been an experienced and proficient hunter back on his birth moon of ₹-593-ॐπ-2-2, the need for his return to the confines of the community were far less pressing that that of the female and her baby. It was ten days before he felt the need to appear in the population center, and only at the word of his Mayan female counterpart did he agree to the blood test.

Aurora informed Tikal a few days later that the last of the Mayans had been located and tested with negative results, and Tikal's response was curious. He said, "You, and others such as Ross, have taught our people how to coexist with you on our birth world and here on Earth. We have come to learn that the process of that is only one aspect of our evolutionary shift, so could this be considered another?"

"What do you mean?"

"The young hunter that all of you have been searching for. He has agreed, in the same way that I did, to have his blood tested for purity."

"That's true, but why would that be evolutionary?"

"Both of us did so at the request of a female."

ʆ

CHAPTER FOURTEEN

ROAD TRIP TO YESTERYEAR

Throughout the several months since constructing their initial prototype vehicle, Colt and Hank had modified the design with a few additions. Chief among those was the installation of a small generator and a dragging brake to the undercarriage, but neither could have been accomplished without the help of their engineering friends at the manufacturing plant.

Extended trial runs under pedal and sail power had proven that the vehicle could withstand any punishment that the less than perfect terrain would present, but the lack of a light source made nighttime operation somewhat risky. The new generator could collect energy harnessed from all three of the vehicles power sources, and store it for use by the newly installed lights on the triangular mainframe whenever the need arose. In keeping with design traditions of various watercrafts from the pre-apocalyptic time on Earth, the mountings were gimbaled. Although that use had normally been reserved for instrumentation, such as a compass, or by the far less vital need of beverage holders, the concept kept the aforementioned level during turbulent conditions. In the current instance, gimbaled lighting would remain focused on the upcoming terrain should the vehicle ever heel over due to an unexpected burst of wind.

With Janet having worked a frantic schedule of research and clinical trials in regard to the virus throughout those same several months, Colt noticed that she was showing signs of fatigue. Given the scope of the monumental task confronting her and other members of the medical community, it was no wonder. Still, Colt felt she needed a break sooner than later. Locating Aurora, he said, "Can you help me convince Janet that she needs to take a break for a few days."

"Sure Colt. I can try, but you know as well as I do that she is extremely dedicated to her task."

"That's true. I do have an idea though, and I think it would be wonderful if you and Tikal joined us on an adventure. With Hank, the five of us could have a nice getaway for a few days. If Janet knew that you were interested, it might be enough to sway her."

"That sounds intriguing, what did you have in mind?"

"Well, it has been a long time since we all took that trip on the shuttle to the museum complex and..."

"Hang on Colt; let me stop you for a second. I don't have any desire to go back to Cheyenne Mountain, and I really don't believe that Janet would want to either. Why don't you and a few of the guys go instead?"

"I appreciate your honesty Aurora, but that's not what I had in mind. Besides, going on some trip with a few of the guys won't help Janet's need for a break."

"That's true. So, what's the plan then?"

"I was thinking that some exploring of the coastal area to the east could provide all of us with a nice diversion, and the SSP vehicle would be the perfect way to do that."

"Sounds like a good idea, but what's the SSP vehicle?"

"That's what Hank has named our prototype. It's short for Sail, Solar, and Pedal."

Two days later, with some prompting from Dr. Halley, Janet took a well-earned break from her duties at the medical labs. With the SSP fully supplied with food, water, and gear for a multi-day trip, Colt and the four passengers climbed onboard for their planned dawn departure. Standing beside the Doctor to see them off, Tori said, "I hope you all have a wonderful adventure, but please be careful. You are important members of our community, and we need you to return safely."

Each of them nodded with agreement, and then Colt said, "Is everybody ready to go? If so, then we all need to start pedaling."

Once clear of the community, a brief stop enabled Hank to raise the mast. Then they followed the shoreline to the east with the wheels running smoothly upon the hard packed sand.

Watching them disappear from view, Dr. Halley turned to Tori and said, "Try not to worry about them too much. Colt and Hank are more experienced with the safe operation of that thing than anyone else. I'm sure they will be fine."

"I hope you're right, but that's not my main concern. Although he had kept the information from Janet so that she would agree to go along on the trip, Colt told me that he wanted to travel for two full days of exploration before beginning the return. If he sticks to that plan, they will be gone for at least three nights."

"True, but they can communicate with us if the need arises, and we could always send a shuttle to pick them up if they run into any problems."

"You're right doctor, but the historical disk recordings have stated that no one has ventured that far to the east from this population center for a few centuries. I have no idea what they might find."

"I think that's why Colt wanted to go out there. For men like him, life is an adventure that needs to be explored."

With the late afternoon sun sinking low to their rear, Colt turned to ask, "Hey Hank, do you think we should stop and set up a camp for the night?"

"Sure dad, how about right up there on that rise?"

Returning his gaze forward to locate where his son was pointing, he replied, "That looks like a good enough place to me. Just let me bring in some sail to slow us down?"

A few moments later Colt applied the new drag brake and the SSP came to a stop so everyone could climb out. As Hank began the procedure of lowering the mast and securing the vehicle, Janet asked, "What can I do to help?"

"I've got this mom, why don't you pick out the spot where can build a fire and camp?"

The request, although innocent enough, reminded Janet of an event that had transpired many years before. It was the first time that she had been asked to pick out a campsite since Robert had done so on the afternoon preceding her abduction by the alien species in 1957. The events of that night had, in a lengthy and inadvertent way, brought Janet to the life that she now led. She quickly shook herself clear of the memory, and after visually surveying the area, walked several yards before turning to Hank and saying, "How about right here?"

Tikal then built a fire at the chosen site within minutes, and the five of them enjoyed a sunset over the coast and stargazing for a few hours afterward. The following morning called for an early departure after breakfast, but Janet was surprised to see Colt climb into the seat beside her. In a pre-planned move, Hank took the helm of the SSP after raising the mast. Turning toward her, Hank winked at his mother and said, "Alright then. Is everybody ready to go?"

Janet looked at Aurora and Tikal, who revealed no visible measure of concern, and then at Colt. He smiled and said, "Did you trust me, and feel safe, while I was driving?"

"Yes, I did."

"Then you should feel even more at ease with Hank at the helm."

"What are you saying Colt? Although I'm aware that the two of you have been working on this project from the beginning, I always thought of Hank as your assistant."

"Well you have been extremely busy during the course of that time, so your position is understandable. It's important for all of us that you alter your way of thinking though. With practice, Hank has become more proficient with the safe operation of the SSP than anyone else, and that includes me."

Colt's point was then proven to be correct throughout the course of the next several hours. While never creating a level of discomfort or uneasiness for his passengers, Hank gave them all a fantastic ride. Moving further from the coast, he maneuvered the vehicle through all types of terrain with a gifted expertise. He demonstrated his ability to quickly adjust both sail deployment and orientation to the wind on countless occasions, and even applied a soft pressure on the drag brake a few times to aid in course correction. Janet, now more visibly relaxed, reached for and grasped Colt's hand. He smiled when she said, "You were right. Hank is very good at this."

"Yes he is, and based on his instinctive feel for the SSP, I think that he would be a natural at something else."

"What's that?"

"We would need to speak with Tori to see if it could even be a possibility, but I think that Hank should go through whatever training is necessary so that he could learn how to fly the shuttle."

Before having a chance to respond, their conversation was interrupted as the vehicle crested yet another rise in the rolling terrain. Hank had apparently noticed something, as he pointed and shouted out, "Hey everybody, look over there."

Instantly intrigued, Colt squinting and said, "That's good spotting at this range Hank, what do you think it is?"

"I don't know, but let's find out."

Without waiting for either a confirming or dissenting word, Hank made the appropriate course correction. Janet then said, "Did you teach him that?"

Colt replied, "Teach him what?"

"To make a decision that could affect all of us without even waiting for a response from you or me."

"No I didn't, but he's learned one aspect of becoming an effective leader. When he is sitting in that chair, he decides what course of action the SSP will take. Besides, Hank knows that we came out here, at least in part, to explore the area."

As they drew closer to the coast, the secret of what Hank had spotted became clear. Although there was very little that still remained, it was obvious that they had stumbled upon the ruins of an ancient city or town. Plant life had overgrown and obscured anything that remained inland, and that included a few mounds that may have been toppled buildings. Along the shoreline a few crumbled outcroppings of long ago habitation were buried deep into the sand, and the waves circulated in and around other objects whose visible tops breached the surface. With the SSP maintaining a slow crawl, Hank said, "Just tell me when you want to stop dad."

Realizing that Hank had relinquished command for the moment, Colt replied, "I will son, but for now just keep trolling."

A short time later, an object protruding from the sand caught their collective eye. It appeared as if it may have been a portion of a large statue, so Aurora asked, "Hank, could you please stop for a minute?"

As they all inspected the object more closely, Aurora placed a hand over her mouth. She felt a sense of recognition toward the work, and began to look around for additional signs of identification. Then after attaining what she believed to be the proper course, she moved away from the group. Tikal hadn't noticed, as he was feeling the strange substance of the statues protruding green arm and hand. Although accustomed to the stone statues around the Mayan sundial used to measure the planting, harvest, and eclipse days on his birth world, this substance was foreign to him. Noticing how captured Tikal had become, Colt leaned over to his friend and said, "This statue was made of something called bronze. It's a type of metal."

Looking up at Colt, Tikal asked, "This is very strange, was it stronger than stone?"

"In this case yes, but that is not always true. This metal statue has withstood the powers of the ocean and sand for many centuries, but bronze is only one form of metal. There are many different types of metal, and some of those are not as strong as some types of stone."

While they were discussing the statue, Janet and Hank had followed Aurora at a respectful distance. When at last she gasped in disbelief and fell to her knees, they shouted for Colt and Tikal while rushing to her side. At the point where the wide sandy beach gave way to intruding fingers of lush vegetation, the corner of a smooth black surface could be easily seen. An emblem of sorts was also partially visible, and Aurora's initial belief from her identification of the statue was verified when she pulled away the vines and dug into the sand.

Hank asked, "What is it Aurora?"

Turning to answer the question, she could see Colt and Tikal quickly approaching. Then she loudly exclaimed, "I think I know exactly where we are!"

Staring at the rather large hole that Aurora had dug in the sand and the now fully visible emblem upon the smooth black surface, Hank asked, "What is that thing?"

"It's supposed to be a depiction of a longhorn Hank. It was one of the several breeds of a fairly large animal that once roamed many parts of the Earth."

"So how do you know that, and why is it here?"

"I think that this is a portion of the top corner of our giant score-board that was located at the south end of the football stadium."

Janet, from her years of living in the state, possessed a minor knowledge of the Texas Longhorn football program. She then asked, "What? Are you sure about that Aurora?"

"Without a doubt, this is part of our scoreboard."

At that moment Colt caught his first glimpse of the easily recogniz-able emblem, and was quick to exclaim, "No way! I can't believe it!"

Hank then knelt beside Aurora in the sand and said, "I don't know what a scoreboard was used for, or what a football stadium is either, but why do you refer to it as our?"

"Because I attended and graduated from this school while my father Ross was working in politics a short distance away. I was lucky enough to attend several football games in this place while doing so, and it's just an old habit for those of us to claim anything associated with the university as ours."

Turning to look at her with amazement, Hank asked, "You mean that this place was once part of a school?"

"Yes it was Hank, but not just any school. We are on ground that was once the campus of the University of Texas, and I spent four years of my life here in the city of Austin."

CHAPTER FIFTEEN
A GEOGRAPHIC LINK

After camping for the night on what was believed, at least in Aurora's mind, to be a section of the former playing surface, the group continued an exploration of the surrounding region on foot. Aurora's discovery had been truly fascinating without a doubt, but her claim that they were indeed within the city of Austin, and on the grounds of the UT campus, required some additional validation. It was possible that the nearby impact, which had completely obliterated the southern portion of her beloved Texas, had simply picked up and thrown the splintered piece of scoreboard several miles to the north with literally thousands of tons of debris. For that matter, an ensuing salvo of giant tsunamis could have created a similar result. There was no way to be definitively sure, and even if other matching debris from the university were located, identifying their exact location would be challenging.

Colt attempted to be the voice of reason in that regard by explaining that possibility while he continued to search for further evidence, but Aurora held firm. She said, "You could be right Colt. We may be nearly two-hundred miles to the north of where Austin once stood and on the campus of TCU in Fort Worth for all that we know, but

I remember exactly what Ross had said during our orbital approach. While identifying and relaying to me the geographic locations of each population center, he did state that an obvious impact had eliminated the southern portion of Texas. He also said that he believed the new coastline was somewhere close to the area of Austin, so I took a closer look myself. Colt, you weren't near the viewing window at that time, but by then the alien vessel had brought us into a lower orbit, and I concurred with Ross."

Realizing that Aurora had recalled the events of that time with clarity, and knowing that Ross was months away from becoming seriously ill when those observations had been made, Colt conceded to her position. He could offer no evidence to dispute their visual claim, so with humbleness befitting Aurora's father and his former boss, he replied, "Fair enough Aurora. If both of you thought that the newly defined coast of Texas runs through where Austin once stood, then that's good enough for me. Perhaps we can uncover some evidence to explain how it happened."

With the subject then temporarily dropped, the group search continued throughout the remainder of the day. A few more bits of evidence were uncovered to help substantiate Aurora's claim, but the real find was a section of marble that contained the name of a campus building that Aurora was familiar with. Additionally, the group theorized that a large cylindrical lump of vegetation may have consumed what little remained of the fallen University tower.

After returning to the nearby campsite of the previous night, Colt said, "I'm sorry that I doubted you Aurora. With the evidence that we have discovered today, I now believe that we are where Austin used to be."

Never wanting to come across with an arrogant voice of knowledge toward her good friend, Aurora gathered herself and said, "Thanks Colt, that's nice of you to say. Now if you don't mind me asking, what do you think happened during the apocalypse to place Austin on the coast?"

"Well, I'm not an expert who could substantiate this theory, but maybe the impact that obliterated a portion of the state also pushed a massive amount of tailings up under where Austin was located. It would explain, in spite of the dramatic rise in the global ocean levels, why this area has become beachfront property."

With that said, Aurora began to reflect on her time as a student at the university, and how she would occasionally walk over to meet her father for lunch. As best as her memory could facilitate, Aurora felt that the adjacent State Capitol Complex must have become a victim of the ocean. Its position, although less than a mile from their current supposed location upon the gridiron, was distant enough, and of a lower overall elevation, to confirm her suspicion. It was probably true that any portion of the humungous steel and marble complex that may have survived the apocalypse was now either completely submerged or had been swallowed up by the sand over time.

The following morning, Hank took the helm of the SSP once again and began following the coast eastward toward home. Although he and Colt had traded seats a few times throughout the ensuing days, by not deviating from the coast for the entirety of the journey, more time was added to the return. At the conclusion of the second full day while under sail in the bright sunlight, the weary group of travelers had covered an extensive amount of territory. As sunset gave way to near darkness, only the distant lights of their home community kept them from setting up camp for an additional night.

Already concerned by the extended duration of their absence with the addition of one night, that now appeared as if it would probably be two, Tori contemplated initiating contact with the SSP to check on their safety. Then word was delivered to her that faint running lights had been spotted moving along the beach to the east.

As Hank pulled softly on the drag brake to halt what little remained of their momentum, he said, "Hello Tori. How are you doing tonight?"

Janet noticed during Tori's response that she didn't seem surprised to see Hank in the driver's seat of the vehicle. Then Janet wondered if she had perhaps been the last person within the community to become aware that her son had developed such a skill. Climbing from her seat,

Janet looked at Tori and said, "This little break was exactly what I needed to rejuvenate, and we all had a great time."

Colt added, "We most certainly did, and the time away for the five of us was wonderful. As a bonus, while we were exploring all that the terrain had to offer, we discovered something very interesting."

Now intrigued, Tori asked, "Really, what did you find?"

"I think that Aurora should be the one to tell you. She made the initial discovery, and then connected the dots by locating additional evidence to prove her thesis."

Turning toward Aurora, Tori then said, "Now I'm really intrigued. Tell me everything Aurora."

"Well I don't have the time to discuss everything right now, but I will tell you this. We discovered a place that holds a direct link to my past life on Earth."

CHAPTER SIXTEEN

SUBTERFUGE

Brittany Cooper, with her infant son cradled safely in her arms, sat quietly while basking in the warmth of another bright and clear sunny day. She had read and studied aspects of what life would be like in Australia during her teenage school years in Montana, and just prior to her abduction by the alien species, was in the final stages of preparation for a year of foreign exchange studies near Sydney. As a consequence of that preparation, Brittany had become as well versed with the surrounding geography and accompanying landmarks as with the culture itself. Although many centuries of Earth time had elapsed since those plans had been suddenly dashed, and the culture radically altered, she felt within her soul that the wait had been worth it. The circumstances of her current situation were vastly different to be sure, but certain aspects of her now living in the land of "down under" for several months beyond her originally intended year were beneficial. Chief among them was that a return to Helena would never be required.

After Brittany's exceedingly long overdue wait, which now included a two day journey within the confines of the shuttle, she, and the remainder of her recruit group, met the administrative team of the population center just moments after their arrival. Although unaware of it at that moment, the man who would become the father of her first child was one of those present during the introductions. While taken on a walking tour throughout their new community, Brittany gazed upon the surrounding terrain and nodded knowingly. Having recognized various landmarks from her memory of both books and film, she turned to one of the female guides, and asked, "What is the name of this community?"

"Our community doesn't have a name."

"It doesn't have a name? How could that be?"

"There was never a need to name our community. For centuries, all of the past and current residents have referred to this place as the population center."

"But every population center, no matter how large or small, must have a name."

"I have studied the available historical disc recordings, and there is no mention of a population center ever having a name after the time of the apocalypse."

"Well if that's true, it's very sad. Many communities before that time were named for famous people. Others areas, such as this one, had more descriptive or unusual names."

"That's interesting. We could add that information to our records if you know what this place was called during your time on old Earth."

"No problem, but can you tell me your name first?"

With a smile, the woman roughly ten years Brittany's senior replied, "My name is Adelaide, and I'm here to help you with any questions that you might have."

Brittany returned the smile and said, "Well it's nice to meet you Adelaide, and thanks for offering to help. As to your question, this community was called Katoomba. This place, along with a few other similar towns, was nestled within the Blue Mountains west of a large city known as Sydney. All of this area was once part of a territory called New South Wales in the country and continent of Australia."

"That's interesting. It's nice that you remembered all of those names, is there anything else that you can tell me?"

Looking to the west from their current position, Brittany added, "Absolutely. All those partially water filled valleys over there were once lined from rim to floor with lush vegetation."

"You seem quite sure; did you live in this area?"

"No, but I had studied Australia extensively, including a large city to the distant southwest of here with the same name as yours. I do however know this particular area of the country very well, as I was about to live close to this place for a year while attending school."

"You said about to? Was it the asteroid apocalypse that stopped you from doing that?"

"No. Something happened to me fifteen years before the asteroid that changed my life forever."

"Fifteen years. What happened to you?"

"I was abducted by the same alien species that brought our entire group back to Earth a few weeks ago."

"Abducted, that's terrible."

"I thought so too at the time, but I soon changed my thinking. I was searching for a way to escape the clutches of my hometown in Montana, but school here in Australia would have been a temporary solution. Soon after I was abducted, I spoke with several other people who had been held for decades, but they had aged very little. I realized that a permanent solution to the problems I faced in Montana had presented itself, so I made some friends with people who knew nothing of my past."

As the walking tour continued, Adelaide pointed out various locations within the population center that would be of importance. Then while showing Brittany the dwelling that she and the other two women in the group would temporarily share, she asked, "Do any of you already have children?"

Brittany was surprised by the question. It was logical to assume that if any of them had been mothers, then their children would be at their side. With that in mind, Brittany replied, "No. We don't have any children yet, but as you are well aware, that will change soon enough. It's the primary reason that our group was sent to this population center."

Unfortunately the statement had been made without verification from her two roommates. Although the woman of Asian descent quickly confirmed that she had no children, the young Mayan woman, in her somewhat broken English said, "I have child back home."

Astonished by the news, Brittany said, "You do?"

Nodding positively, the Mayan replied, "Yes. My boy had seen seven eclipse cycles before our King sent me away with the others to come with you."

"Did Ross or Aurora know that you had a child?"

"Our King said to not tell them."

"Not tell them! How could you keep that a secret?"

"Our King said to not tell them."

"Aren't you angry at your King for saying that?"

"I'm never angry at our King. It is his will that I have other babies here, so that is what I will do."

Adelaide quickly asked, "What is a King, and even more importantly, why does such a person have the power to tell a woman to leave her child behind?"

Brittany replied, "That's complicated, but at one time they were absolute rulers. Although few of the Kings within my era of human evolution had such power, this woman descends from a different time. Her belief system, based on an earlier culture, maintained that a Kings will was the final word on any subject. Those decisions, just or not, were unquestioned. If she challenged her Kings will, she could have been put to death."

"Put to death?"

"Yes. Sadly, there were too many examples of such mistreatment within the history of Earth's past, and some of those practices continued up to the time of the apocalypse. Please don't misunderstand me. Mankind, as an entity, had been evolving beyond that negative aspect, but there was a long way to go before we could have attained the harmonious level enjoyed by the global community of this era. Believe me Adelaide, you should consider yourself blessed to have never either witnessed or experienced such mistreatment."

While settling into her new routines, Brittany realized that the population center with no name had, inadvertently or not, stumbled upon a perfect location for a settlement. She and Adelaide became good friends, and they shared as much information about their respective times on Earth as possible. That included their various experiences and knowledge of men, so during one such interaction, Adelaide, while motioning over Brittany's shoulder said, "What can you tell me about him?"

Turning to see the man that she spoke of, Brittany then replied, "Oh that's Joseph, and he's a nice guy. He, and a group of his friends, were all abducted while flying their planes near Florida in 1945. Janet introduced me to him on the alien ship not long after my abduction in 2007 and that's when I learned from all of them that our collective ageing process had been slowed down considerably. Sixty-two years in captivity, and the man looked to be about thirty. I've spoken to him occasionally throughout the years since that day, and he's always friendly. I guess he's closer to forty by now, but he still looks good."

"Does he interest you?"

"No, he's not my type. Besides, I've got someone else in mind to father my first child."

Now, sixteen months after that conversation, Adelaide and Joseph were the parents of a three month old baby girl. Brittany had given birth to her son a few months prior to that happy event, and now sat with him in relaxed comfort on her favorite hilltop perch. She was now expecting again, and while waiting for the arrival of the man who would soon become that child's father, she gazed eastward. Her distant view included what little remained of the once proud and glistening Sydney skyline that now breeched the surface of the Pacific Ocean. The scene was beautiful with a few tiny islands also visible on this magnificent day, but Brittany was saddened that the Pacific had engulfed most of the rolling hills that had once been home to the Sydney suburbs.

How she had arrived at such a beautiful location had been the byproduct of a quickly developed, yet ingenious, plan that had, against all odds, worked to perfection. When Brittany had overheard Ross informing Aurora of the respective light sources he had observed during the multiple orbit approach to Earth, she instantly took notice. When she then heard Ross ask their alien host if they could set the transport ship down near the light source in what he knew to be Texas, she realized that the site was a long way from her intended final destination. Brittany needed to ensure that she would be relocated to the site along the southeastern coast of Australia, and that would require a measure of deceit on her part.

During the present moment, Brittany smiled devilishly while flashing back to how quickly she had put the formulated plan into action. Via meticulous observation throughout the six week voyage from ₹-593-ऊπ-2-2, Brittany had noticed that Janet nearly always kept an eye on her husband Colt. The trait of insecurity was something that she had never witnessed within the normally strong willed and independent Janet, but the presence of young attractive women in Colt's vicinity had brought it on. The ten young Mayan women on board, sent by their King for no other purpose than to appease Ross and the "Sky God" by acts of propagating the species, must have been driving Janet crazy. The same could probably be said for the other women on the manifest, as they had collectively become a threat to Janet's comfort zone. Brittany knew that the trait Janet exhibited was something that most people had, or would, experience at some point in their lives, and saw it as nothing more than a temporary weakness that must be exploited. With that knowledge in mind, Brittany had intentionally positioned herself as close to Colt as possible on several occasions.

When landing on Earth then became imminent, Brittany used the most simplistic language and tone of voice that she could muster while shouting, "Oh my God. I'm so happy that this trip is almost over, I could just kiss somebody!"

Janet had heard the comment, and spun around just in time to watch Brittany wrap her arms around the neck of an unsuspecting Colt, and while firmly pressing against him, deliver a passionate kiss. Her well planned action produced the exact response that Brittany had hoped for, as even though she had no desire to ever kiss him again, Colt gave her a little smile while pushing her away. Janet on the other hand, showed a different facial expression, and Brittany knew that those few seconds of artificial passion with Colt had effectively pissed her off. That would most probably ensure getting herself shipped off to a distant location, but Brittany would need to further manipulate the situation so that she would be sent to Australia.

A few days later, when the time came for the selection process of phase two, Brittany decided her best approach would be to request one or two specific population centers as her preferred destination choices. She would need to make those choices seem plausible for a woman who had grown up in the colder northern latitudes, and did so while understanding that Janet would conspire with Aurora to ensure that each of her requests would also be denied. With a tone of self-bravado, Brittany announced, "I would really like to go to the site Ross spotted in either England or Western Canada."

Brittany's belief that a pact between Janet and Aurora would form was instantly verified when Aurora replied, "We can't accommodate your requests Brittany. The recruit groups for each of those locations have already been selected."

Knowing that the statement was nothing more than a fabrication, Brittany drove the point home by adding, "Oh, I didn't know that Aurora. I'm sorry; I was under the impression that the selection process just began. If those locations aren't available, then perhaps I could stay here in this group with you."

In the momentary silence that followed, Brittany hoped that she hadn't been too forceful. Overplaying her hand could cause the plan to backfire, and there might not be anyway to recover. While wishing for the best possible outcome, her internal voice kept repeating, "Not India or Africa. Please, don't send me to India or Africa." Then she heard the words she was hoping for, as Janet said, "Actually Brittany, we think that you would make a nice addition to the group heading to what was formerly Australia."

With an excellent poker face so as not to expose her joy, she softly uttered, "Australia, but that's so far away."

"We know that Brittany, but each recruit is accepting a certain level of sacrifice in order to serve the greater good of our species. You were made aware of that fact back on our former home moon before you signed up, and being placed within a group bound for Australia is your particular sacrifice."

Her plan had worked perfectly, and Brittany realized she could probably outplay Janet anytime that the need arose. All she had to do was imply a romantic or sexual intention toward Colt, and Janet would lose control of her objective thinking. While once again subduing any expression of her true inner joy, Brittany solemnly replied, "Alright Janet. I understand, and of course you're right. Each of us must do what is best for the collective good."

CHAPTER SEVENTEEN
PERSONALIZATION

Near the conclusion of the second year, after having grown weary of identifying the majority of the communities by nothing more than the numbers of one through sixteen, Aurora initiated what she and others felt to be a necessary change. There had been a time when, as one would expect, each population center believed that their location was the focal point of the Earth, if not the universe. Employing the communication system of that time many centuries before, a lottery had been held to establish the currently used random pattern to the numbering system. The result was less than ideal in the minds of many, but in the time since, it had never been altered. The site within the former British Isles, much to the collective dismay of its citizens', had been known as number sixteen since that time. Meanwhile, the smaller community in West Africa had drawn number one.

Aurora never felt at ease with the random numbering system that didn't allow for grouping according to geographic proximity. She believed that locations such as Eastern Australia and New Zealand should have neighboring numbers of five and six, but those sites were actually numbers five and thirteen. Brittany had convinced many within her community to refer to their location by its former name of Katoomba as opposed to the less colorful number five. That process of socialization had begun shortly after her arrival, but no other population center had received a similar effort from any within their group of recruits. In more recent months Colt had used his influence within the old Pacific Northwest to bring about additional change, as those located within the small community east of Vancouver's ruins had begun to refer to themselves as citizens of Maple Ridge. Aurora wished to move forward with a personalization effort for each of the remaining fourteen sites, and sought out the blessings of respective local administrative teams to do that. Incorporating the technology of Earth's orbiting satellite system to pinpoint exact locations of each population center, and communicating with various recruits who had maintained some knowledge of old Earth geography, she was able to quickly identify appropriate names for each.

Adding to the list of the already established Katoomba and Maple Ridge, La Calera on the west coast of South America quickly replaced number ten. Then Aurora renamed her current location of number three. The discovery of what had once been Austin during the eastward exploration on the SSP had helped to provide their exact distance to the west, so a name was easy to determine. In honor of the township that had once occupied the space before the asteroid apocalypse, the population center where the recruits had been deposited back on Earth was officially dubbed as Dripping Springs.

A few small population centers, such as Whitecliffs in New Zealand were named in similar fashion, while those located in the former vacant areas between large cities, took on a hybrid classification. The most noteworthy example of such naming occurred within the former South American country of Brazil, as number six, the largest of the communities, was named Rio Paulo. Although not the most endearing of titles, those citizens within the former British Isles were pleased that they no longer would be saddled with number sixteen. As descendants of a long ago society who had placed significant stock in their perceived social standing and birthright, having the final number of any set diminished their self-worth. With collective relief, they assumed the name of Crewe within the ever shrinking global community.

With each community then in receipt of a personalized touch, Tori turned to Aurora and said, "I must admit, this was unexpected. I didn't know until recently that you could look beyond numbers and data. I've worked with you for eighteen months now, and I thought you had embraced our centuries old method of numbering each population center.

Aurora offered a smile, and replied, "I can understand why you would think that Tori. On the surface, the numbering system would appear to be the kind of thing that I would love, but not when it involves communities. I'm aware that some people believe that this process was a ridiculous exercise, but not me. In spite of a lifelong love of numbers and data, even I know that life needs a reprieve from it occasionally. Not everything should have a number attached to it."

"Now your words are matching your actions Aurora. It's a very enlightened approach, but why the change of heart?"

"Thanks. I guess it's because in every population center people are falling victim to the virus, and at this point in time, we haven't figured out a way to stop it. I believe that most people would want the record to not only indicate some personal information about them, but also where they lived their life. I don't know about you Tori, but I prefer to die in Dripping Springs as opposed to number three."

ꝓ

CHAPTER EIGHTEEN
PIN CUSHIONS

As the third complete year since their return to Earth came to a close, Aurora's records of placement showed that ninety-four of the reproduction recruits had held true to their collective promissory effort of revitalizing the dying gene pool of Earth. It was hoped that sometime several years into the future both Hank and Kristyn, as numbers ninety-five and ninety-six, would also find suitable mates for the same purpose. As for the current time, their respective levels of physiological maturity prevented them from such consideration.

The records for year one were unable to provide an accurate measuring stick of potential progress, as the majority of the few births and deaths had taken place during the later stages of the timeframe. Files for each of the recruits, and their respective offspring, had then been updated at the conclusion of the second year, and once again to close the third. Sadly, those same records, while providing a complete and accurate measurement, had also drawn a bleaker global picture. They revealed that throughout the same timeframe, far too many deaths as a consequence of the virus had offset the population gains attained as a byproduct of the revitalization process.

Although it had shown early promise, the attempted genetic enrichment would prove to be a most daunting task for many years to come. Optimism remained high among many, but there was only so much that could be done with a full term human pregnancy exceeding nine months in duration. Even so, it became critical to accelerate the program efforts.

Each of the fifty-two adult males, including Colt and Tikal, had now been responsible for the fathering of a child with, at a minimum, three women within their respective communities. As for the adult female recruits, each of the forty-two had delivered at least one child. Slightly over half of them, including Natiya and Brittany had given birth to a second. The ten Mayan women, per the parting instructions of their King, had taken to the assigned task with enthusiasm. They had been ordered to produce children on the new world, and each had willingly fulfilled that directive by producing two offspring. Three of them, with no desire to potentially anger their King or the "Sky God", were already expecting yet another.

Unfortunately, Aurora did not live long enough to see the completion of the third year. After a difficult battle with the virus, she finally succumbed in the exact gruesome fashion as each of the other associated victims. If any positive came from the lengthy knowledge of her eventual demise, it was the ability to take appropriate measures with regard to her meticulous record keeping. The choice to carry on the responsibility of the work had been obvious to Aurora, and Natiya gladly accepted both the invitation and challenge. In so doing, Natiya's only request was to include Kristyn in the training process. Her thinking, shared by many others, was that she and her eldest daughter could combine their efforts, as has been recently accomplished, to cover the task for many years to come. That path was logical, as Natiya had, just like every other person over thirty on the planet, tested positive for the virus. Kristyn, now ten years old, had once again come back with negative test results, so she would theoretically continue the process when Natiya could no longer do so.

The funeral service for Aurora, a full six months into the past, had been performed with less fanfare than the one for Ross two years prior.

Perhaps that was due to her being less of a public figure than her father, or perhaps the cause was an ever increasing amount of funeral services for the many that had fallen. Whatever the case, Aurora was laid to rest next to Ross and Gabriela while fulfilling a promise she had made to her father during the days of her childhood. She was lowered into a small rise overlooking the ocean while cloaked in the American flag that had once covered the coffin of her grandfather Robert.

Hank, who was nearly eleven at the time, saluted the flag as he had been taught by Colt for Ross's service. Then turning to his father he said, "That was a cool promise that Ross and Aurora had with each other about being cloaked in their respective grandfathers' military flags. Were you aware of that promise before Aurora asked us to do it for her last week?"

"Yes I was. Ross had spoken with me about it years ago, and he wanted me to ensure that the ritual was carried out in case Aurora never had a chance to discuss it with anyone."

Janet, with tears welling in her eyes at having lost the only grand-daughter that she ever knew, intervened by saying, "Our family only has the one remaining flag now. Do either of you have any future plans for it?"

Hank replied, "I don't know if you remember mom, but when we discovered the flag in the exhibit for Ross at the Cheyenne Mountain museum, he asked Aurora to keep it safe with the two that have now been used. About six months ago she asked me if I would continue to care for it after she was gone, so I promised her that I would. Unless you or dad has another idea, I would like to protect this flag for my entire life."

While rubbing her eyes dry, Janet said, "I think that's a great idea Hank. Perhaps one day you can pass on the legacy of the flag to one of your children."

"That's a deal mom, I promise."

With Aurora's death came the realization that Tikal was now the oldest living citizen of Dripping Springs. The consensus was that he also held that distinction globally, but not every citizen had been accounted for in the six months since he had been labeled as such. A handful of the infected elderly in both the South American settlement of La Calera, and the community of Whitecliffs on the former south island of New Zealand, had since relocated to the solitude of the mountains. Their status was currently unknown, but it was doubtful that any of them had survived very long with the potential harshness of exposure to the wilderness, or the grip of the virus.

Throughout the two year timeframe since Aurora had stumbled upon the theory that Tikal and the twenty other Mayan's were somehow immune to the virus, her belief had become more plausible. As the age of those around them that became infected and died continued to plummet, each of the Mayan citizens repeatedly tested negative. Categorized as a medical miracle, Tikal and the others continued to be treated as if they were giant pin cushions. It was fair to estimate that they had given several pints each throughout the course of multiple small doses, as many samples of their untainted blood had been scrutinized in labs throughout the globe. Then beginning with the most advanced cases, a small amount of their blood had been cross matched and injected directly into the bloodstream of those infected. That process, due to no tangible results, then proceeded backwards to those patients who were younger or less advanced with their symptoms. Eventually even those in their thirties who, based on their age and Janet's early findings, still had perhaps several years of viral gestation before death, failed to show any signs of eradication.

Throughout the entire process, only five patients of the several thousand that were tested exhibited a positive reaction to the treatment. That reaction, although subtle at first, was shared by Janet, Brittany, and the three pilots who had volunteered as recruits from the larger group of fourteen abductees of Flight 19 in 1945. Deciphering their commonality was easy, as Janet knew that both she and Brittany had also been abducted by the alien species. Although each of the five had been exposed and infected for over three years, tests had proven that when compared to that of other patients, the battery of minute blood transfusions they had received had effectively slowed the progression of the virus to a crawl. In Janet's case, the results of her blood testing were the most baffling to the medical community. Aside from being older than any of the other four, she had also been more closely exposed to patient zero for several months before his death.

When Dr. Halley asked, "Janet, do you have a theory as to why the five of you have reacted so differently to the experimental testing?"

She responded, "Well, I think that there must be some correlation to our abduction by the alien species. After all, we, and each of the more than two hundred other long term abductees had our ageing process slowed to a crawl while in their captivity. Only after being released at the conclusion of our six week transport, when we inadvertently became part of the pilgrimage effort on ₹-593-૩ᴗπ-2-2, did we begin to age again at the normal rate. I just don't believe that having the virus slow to a crawl in a similar fashion within only our five systems is a coincidence."

"Well, that does seem like a logical place to start. Are you five the only ones still alive?"

"I can't answer that doctor. I have no way of knowing what has become of our colony back on that moon, but we are the only five abductees who returned to Earth."

CHAPTER NINETEEN

DEFLATED SOUL

Another year had rolled past, and the global death rate curve steepened. The year had been difficult in many respects for each population center, and the toll of those circumstances weighed heavily upon Janet's soul. Her frustrations within the medical lab also continued, as no significant progress toward viral abatement, or a preventative vaccine, had been achieved. Adding to that level of frustration was the loss of the man she had worked with so closely in seeking said cure. A few months after the completion of the third year since Janet's return to Earth, Dr. Halley passed away due to the virus. During his final weeks he had been of absolutely no use in the lab, as prolonged episodes of his severe hallucinations exceeded those of Ross. Although Janet maintained the ability to communicate with other research personnel for potential breakthroughs, she and the Dripping Springs labs had been hampered by the loss of their most senior and well versed mind.

Of more significant damage to Janet's normally stern resolve was the loss of Colt, as he had also fallen prey to the virus six months after the doctor. For those within Dripping Springs, or in a broader sense, the global community, the loss was tremendous. Not to diminish the passing of other citizens, but Colt was one of the few who could offer an important link to Earth's former civilization. Aside from the introduction of what would develop into the SSP, or the hybrid variations of it, he continued to couple modern technological advancements with those of the past to enhance future achievements.

One example of that mindset was the introduction of wind turbines as an additional power generating source. Colt had certainly not invented the concept, nor did he assume any credit for having done so, but the idea had proved most useful for the various population centers. Since construction of the Dripping Springs prototype more than two years before his death, dozens of turbines had been built around the planet. Maple Ridge had been the first community to embrace the wind turbine concept for their rugged terrain, and had subsequently worked closely with Colt when developing other uses.

Another addition to the concept of sail power involved the team of scientists dedicated to the exploration of space. Already possessing the ability to send and retrieve small solar powered probes that had been studying Mars or Venus, they were constantly searching for a way to speed up the process of the long round trips. Colt saw that as an opportunity, so he approached a man who represented the modern day version of NASA. Then he asked, "Have you thought of using a large sail to harness more of the suns energy for your space probes?"

Colt knew instantly that his question wasn't a foolish one, as a slight lifting of the scientists eyebrows indicated that the man was intrigued by the thought. Then Colt heard him say, "That's an interesting concept. Can you elaborate for me?"

"Well, I can try. I won't claim to know too much about the process, but prior to the apocalypse, NASA and other space agencies were working on the concept. In simple terms they would equip a probe or other vehicle with a sail that would unfurl once it left orbit, and then capture what was referred to as the solar wind. The idea was that the probe would gain additional speed in the vacuum of space."

"That's very interesting. Was it ever tested?"

"To tell you the truth, I'm not sure. As I said, I don't know too much about it. I'm sure that Ross would have known, but it's just one of those conversations that we never had."

"Well I know that a few of our scientists would be very interested in discussing the concept, and whatever you could offer as information would be most helpful."

"Sure, whatever I can do to help."

With that Colt somehow became an honorary member of the group responsible for space endeavors, and he made sure that Hank was also an integral part of the process. Although neither Colt nor Hank could offer much science to the collective think tank, he felt that the learning opportunity for Hank was too great to pass up. Besides, the invitation to the round table discussions wouldn't have occurred if their experience in both the development of the SSP and their actual space flight wasn't considered to be a valuable addition to the project.

Within months, the first pair of what would become several probes were launched toward each of the neighboring two planets with a newly developed solar sail. As Colt had initially described in rough detail, the protruding fifty-foot sail was unfurled after each of the probes cleared the atmosphere. Both probes then completed their respective roundtrip journeys in less time than any previous ventures, but the solar sail burned up on re-entry into Earth's atmosphere. The ensuing generation of probes had been enhanced to allow for the sails to retract before entering Earth's atmosphere, and Colt had lived long enough to witness their triumphant returns.

From a more intimate perspective, Colt's death was devastating for Janet. He had been the man that she fell in love with long after being ripped away from her family and life by the alien species, and they had developed a true partnership of souls during the challenging years on ₹-593-ꝛπ-2-2. Their partnership had also created Hank, and Colt had been a most wonderful father. He was not only supportive of Hank's every interest, but Colt also provided him with constant opportunities to broaden his outlook and education through practical life application. That attention was most evident in how Colt had also inspired the creative engineering side of Hank's personality. By encouraging expanded thought toward embracing what the advances of new Earth's technology might provide for other inventions, Colt hoped that would inspire Hank to eventually achieve greatness as Ross had predicted. Colt also helped Hank develop personal relationships with those of all ages, and freely included him in the advanced discussions or projects that one might initially believe to be beyond the scope of the young man's comprehension.

Hank's development also included profound external influences such as Megan Crenshaw who taught him about strength of character and the value of hard work and ethical behavior. Or, how to remain humble when placed in a position of leadership as demonstrated time and again by both Ross and Jessica. Those traits had been instrumental in the shaping of their son, and therefore Janet believed that Hank had already achieved greatness. Her thoughts of such things went beyond a mother's normal feelings of pride toward her own child. They were amplified by Hank's unparalleled mastery of the SSP, and the more recent and impressive way, at the tender age of twelve, that his two years of training had made him one of the more reliable shuttle pilots in Dripping Springs.

During a lengthy solitary walk on the beach, Janet reflected on how much the loss of Colt, and others, had taken out of her. She also realized that she would be forever thankful for the type of young man that Hank was becoming as a byproduct of what each of those people had instilled upon him. The weight of all that surrounded her was in desperate need of release, so after turning in a complete circle to ensure that she couldn't be seen, Janet plopped herself down on the sand and began to cry.

Her thoughts soon turned to how their old alien friend might be able to assist with the new trouble facing Earth, but unfortunately he had never been seen or heard from since departing for his home world. As he was the one responsible for informing Ross about the need for genetic enrichment on Earth, Janet thought it was strange that the alien had never returned to check on the progress of the program.

Silently expressing her desire to see the alien again, Janet also hoped that he would return to Earth and provide assistance toward their desperate endeavor. What she was unaware of at the time, was that her internal voice had been heard across the vastness of the cosmos.

CHAPTER TWENTY
THE HIGH COUNCIL

Approaching the high council of the exploratory fleet with the obligatory escort at his side, the alien who had come to know Ross and his collective so well gave the seven members a respectful bow. After receiving telepathy to explain why he had requested an audience with them, his own telepathic reply was, "I have some important information to share with you."

"From our perspective that is stating the obvious. No one ever comes before us with information that isn't believed to be of importance. I will remind you that we, as the high council, will determine if you possess important information."

"I understand."

"Excellent, now what information do you wish to share with the high council?"

"I have just received a telepathic request from one of the humans on ₹-829-ʒ∪π-3, or Earth, as they call it. She was one of over two-hundred of our long term abductees many Earth centuries ago before the apocalypse interfered with that experimental process. I believe that she has now become the first of her species to develop long range telepathic abilities."

After a brief moment of exclusion while the high council communicated with each other, the leader replied, "You are correct brother, as that information is of importance to the high council. Now, you claim that she had a request of you?"

"Yes she did. She is requesting that I return to monitor their progress on ₹-829-૨π-3. It seems that her species needs help with a problem that they are unable to resolve."

After referencing their operational schematics, the leader of the council replied, "The rotations for monitoring the evolutionary progress of certain species are currently underway in another sector of the quadrant. I'm afraid that system ₹-829 will not be viewed again for quite some time."

Having learned from Ross and others within the group of humans that the need for political correctness may be one of but a few true universal constants, his response was carefully crafted. "I understand this is an unusual request of the council, and I welcome your guidance. With your permission I wish to depart immediately on a special mission to ₹-829-૨π-3."

"Immediately, can you give the council a reason why?"

"Yes I can. You are aware that although time is linear, not all systems, or even the various species upon a planet or moon within a system, have the same base unit for measuring that time."

"Yes, I'm aware of that."

"Well, in this instance the timeline moves very quickly on ₹-829-૨π-3. During the six weeks of human time that were necessary to travel from ₹-593-૨π-2-2 to their home world, the planet completed thirty-five revolutions around the host star."

"And your point is?"

"The human species is on the brink of a huge step forward in their evolutionary process. The female who sent the request for help is proof of that. I'm unsure as to what their problem is at this moment, but if we wait several years of Earth time before our normal observational rotations, then everything that we have worked for may be lost."

"You present a strong argument, and your point is well taken. Now, do you have a plan of action to present?"

"Our home world is much closer to ₹-829-ง兀-3 than system ₹-593 is. I could take two crew members with me in one of the newly developed fast long range scout ships, and traverse the distance to Earth in just a few of their years."

"Your proposal is understood. We will deliberate."

During the course of that debate, the newest member of the high council also reviewed the operational history of system ₹-829 from his position at the end of the bench. Then when asked his opinion by the leader of the council, he replied, "Our brother who stands before us, like me, carries a special interest in this project. The archives indicate his involvement with prior monitoring of Earth as they call it, and with leading the most recent of the four relocations of the dominant species to ₹-593-ง兀-2-2. He also led the mission to retrieve a few of them and return that group to ₹-829-ง兀-3."

"I see. So you believe that his qualifications justify our consideration for him to proceed?"

"Yes number one, I do."

"And that we should grant his request immediately?"

"Yes number one, I do."

After another moment of deliberation, the council leader then projected, "We agree with your assessment number seven. As you possess such belief in our brother's abilities, then we feel you should be the one to grant him the mission. In so doing, be aware of the fact that his actions reflect upon this council. As you are his sponsor, you may experience some repercussions if he should fail."

"I understand number one. However, in the absence of failure, there should be praise for our brother if he succeeds in salvaging our long term objective for ₹-829-ง兀-3."

Upon receiving the subsequent blessings of the council from the member to his farthest left, the alien glanced over and recognized his former supervisor. It had been a long time since he had been a member of that alien's command, and had observed, among several others, system ₹-829. It was during one such rotational tour that the two of them experienced an accidental encounter, and the near tragedy that ensued, with two of the few humans to ever walk upon the now non-existent moon of ₹-829-૩ण-3.

The memory of meeting the human Ross for the first time was crystal clear. How Ross had then offered assistance in saving the life of an alien, only moments after witnessing the death of his own companion Dennis, was inspirational. That wounded alien was most fortunate that a minor piece of equipment, which was previously needed for the survival of the dead human astronaut, had been able to spare his life. Without it, he would never have eventually become the most recently appointed member of the high council.

Maintaining his gaze toward his former supervisor seated at the high council bench, the alien whom Janet had communicated with projected toward all seven of them, "I have maintained a special interest with the project of Earth since the time of my first visitation, and wish to see it through. I thank each of you for granting my request."

૬

CHAPTER TWENTY-ONE

MYSTERIOUS MESSAGE

Janet bolted upright from her mat on the floor, as an unexpected voice boomed loudly within her head. Then while searching her surroundings in an attempt to locate the source, a wave of confusion followed. There was no one in the room, but the voice of her old alien friend sounded as if he was standing just a few feet from her. Janet wondered if the experience was nothing more than a harmless dream, but simultaneously hoped that it wasn't something that could be far worse. Had the virus finally caught up with her? Had she entered the dreadful hallucination phase that every other victim of the virus had faced near the end? She knew that she needed to get a grip before paranoia completely took over, but her current foggy state created a momentary challenge in that regard. Although the concise message of the voice didn't make much sense to her, Janet realized that if it was indeed authentic, then it must have been telepathic in origin. She had heard, "Janet, I have received your request for assistance and am departing. We should arrive at your planet within a few of your Earth years."

Later that same morning, while attempting to enjoy a relaxed breakfast with Hank, Janet said, "I'm somewhat hesitant to discuss this, but the strangest thing happened to me earlier this morning."

With nothing more than a passing interest, Hank asked, "Why, what happened to you?"

"I was awakened from a sound sleep when I heard a very strong thought projection from our old alien friend."

Now noticeably intrigued, Hank lifted his gaze from the engineering sketches that he had borrowed and said, "Really? Is he here? Has he come back to check on our progress?"

"I don't think that he's here, but he may be on his way. The thought projection was strange, and didn't specify if he would be checking on our progress."

"May be on the way? Didn't specify? Come on mom, there must be more to it than that."

"Well, his message claimed that he had received my request for assistance and he would arrive in a few Earth years."

"Would arrive in a few years? That doesn't sound like the way he has communicated with any of us in the past."

"I agree, and that's why I'm concerned. The message may have been a dream, but what if I just experienced the first instance of my eventual hallucination phase of the virus?"

"Well, maybe you were dreaming, but I haven't seen you exhibit any behavior suggesting that you are moving into the hallucination phase. As Ross or dad would have said, we need more evidence before jumping to that conclusion. Of course they would also explore another possibility."

"What do you mean?"

"Well, maybe our old alien friend did communicate with you. Just because he has always sent his thought projections toward each of us while in close proximity, it doesn't mean that he can't communicate from a greater distance."

"That's logical I suppose, but as you just said, we need more evidence to validate your thesis. Besides, even if the alien were capable of long distance projection, why contact me?"

"Why wouldn't he contact you? He is aware of our societal structure. With Ross, Gabriela, Aurora, and even dad having passed on, it would be logical to think of you as the leader of our group."

"I have never claimed that position or responsibility."

"I know that, but maybe the alien just assumed it."

"If that's true, then it explains why he contacted me. There is still the question of his message content though. I haven't spoken to him since right before his departure the day after he deposited all of us here. Why would he project that he received my request for assistance?"

"I don't know mom, but as Aurora would have said, we should review the available data."

"What do you mean?"

"Think back to that farewell discussion. Did you request anything from him that may have been interpreted as a need for assistance when, or if, he returned to Earth?"

"I don't think so. I remember joining Ross and others in thanking him for everything that his species had done to help ensure our survival, but nothing more. Then I hadn't given our old friend another thought until yesterday."

"What happened yesterday to make you think of him?"

"I was sitting on the beach thinking about all that has transpired recently, and that he might be able to..."

After her abrupt stop, and the long pause that followed, Hank snapped his fingers next to Janet's face and asked, "Might be able to do what mom?"

Startled back into the reality of the present moment, Janet gulped and replied, "Help us with defeating the virus!"

"Really, well that's interesting!"

"What is? You don't actually believe that he heard my request do you?"

"Sure I do. We have been showed numerous times that the abilities of their species are extremely advanced?"

"That's true enough, but I was told by many of those dying throughout the early struggles upon our former home moon that they had prayed for help and the alien species had not responded to their plea."

"Maybe their message wasn't properly delivered."

"You mean they weren't asking the right questions?"

"Or the correct entity, but that's a different discussion. No, I was thinking that perhaps there is another reason."

"What are you getting at Hank?"

"The timing of your experience is just too coincidental. What you heard last night shows us that the alien species can theoretically receive and project from a great distance."

"That's true I suppose."

"And you have just stated that many others besides you have asked for help that was never granted."

"That's also true."

"Why do you think that is mom?"

"I don't know."

"Well I think it's possible, however unlikely in our belief system, that you have developed an ability that none of those other people possessed."

"What are you saying?"

"Mom, I think that the reason our old friend heard you, and not the others, was because you telepathically projected your thoughts toward him."

ξ

CHAPTER TWENTY-TWO

TRANSITIONS

Throughout each population center, nearly everyone over the tender age of twenty had become either infected by, or dead, as a result of the virus. In truth only about a thousand over thirty were still alive and just four more beyond the age of forty. Now six years since their return to Earth, it appeared that the selective set of four would continue to outlive many of those that were younger. If their current state of good health remained the same, there was no reason to believe that they wouldn't become five in the near future. The youngest of the three Flight 19 pilots, and the fourth of the five long term abductees within the group of recruits, would reach the age of forty in less than a year. In so doing he would then join Tikal, who continued to test negative for the virus, Janet, and his two flying companions as the only souls of that less than advanced age to still be breathing.

Within Dripping Springs, the recent death of Natiya, at only thirty-seven, had become another reminder of how the young continued to perish. Now with the exception of Tikal and Janet, her passing had reduced the high end of the age scale in that population center by another year.

As a recruit, Natiya had most certainly done her part in providing offspring for the gene enrichment program. Aside from Kristyn, who had been born on ₹-593-ૐπ-2-2, Natiya had given birth to three children from different fathers during the first four years since her return to Earth. Unfortunately the youngest of those three, her first and only son, never had the chance to know his mother with great detail. Everyone around her had known that Natiya was within her final days, and luckily for the children her hallucination phase had been mild. Still, she hung on fiercely to the last. Natiya stayed alive long enough to witness little Yuri celebrate his second birthday with friends and family, but within a week of that joyous event she was gone. With each of the three respective fathers having previously succumbed to the virus, her death left Kristyn, now thirteen, with added weight. While still a child on the verge of young womanhood, the role of parent was added to that of older sister for the latest in the long line of orphans.

Several mothers within the community, including Janet, had been mindful and supportive of Kristyn's plight. Collectively that group of women had done whatever they could to assist the young lady, as she was also beginning to experience the challenges associated with her own physiological changes into early womanhood. The combined transitions would be most difficult for anyone to handle, but Kristyn was aware of that. Not only would she be responsible for her own well-being, but the complex and unenviable task of caring for three younger siblings, aged five, four, and two, had also fallen upon her.

Kristyn's situation was also proven to be unique within Dripping Springs. Although she was an orphan herself, no other such person had been left to care for other orphans. Knowing that every previous young orphan in the community had been absorbed into the fold of neighboring families, Janet felt Kristyn deserved the same consideration. While providing a supportive hug, Janet said, "Kristyn, I want you to know that you, and your little sisters and brother, are welcome to live with Hank and I if you wish. We will find a way to make room for you."

"Thanks Janet. Your offer would provide great comfort, but I think that we should stay in our dwelling for the time being. I have been helping my mother with many of the daily tasks for quite some time, and the little one's each have their various routines. I believe that the added shock of transplanting them to another location right now would make things more difficult for them than they already are."

"Alright Kristyn, that's fair enough. I admire you for the strength you are exhibiting, and it's nice that you want to keep things as normal as possible for yourself and the little ones. My offer still stands for you to come by our place as often as you wish, and please don't hesitate to ask for help if you need it."

"Thanks again. I'm sure there will be many things I need help with that I haven't even thought of yet, and I promise to come see you as the need arises."

"That's good Kristyn, but don't feel you can only come by when you need help. I have always thought of you and your mother as friends, and there is no reason that you and I can't continue to build upon that."

From that moment forward the primary concern for Kristyn became the welfare of her younger siblings. She made sure that the basics of nutrition and rest were covered, along with their needs for fresh air and exercise. For each of those aspects, she could roughly follow the patterns that had already been established by her mother. As to the importance of their education, and hers for that matter, Kristyn knew that help from external influences would be required.

With that in mind, Kristyn realized that a wonderful opportunity could exist within Janet's open ended invitation. Whenever she took the little ones to visit with Janet and Hank, Kristyn set a positive example for them by sitting down to learn whatever she could. While she received instruction from Janet on medical terminology or how to treat various injuries, Hank would occasionally quiz the little ones with games involving geography or rudimentary mathematics.

On one such occasion Janet asked, "Kristyn, you have been working very hard to create a positive environment for your sisters and brother, but have you dedicated any time or energy to yourself?"

"Not really. It hasn't been a high priority."

"Well, I think that you should. You know I can watch the little ones, and you could probably use some time alone or with others closer to your age."

"I suppose that would be a nice diversion, and I will probably accept your offer soon. I would like to spend more time with Hank if possible. We have such a good friendship, and I would hate to see that slip away from neglect."

CHAPTER TWENTY-THREE

UNWELCOME DISCOVERY

The voice was in her head again, and while losing sleep because of it, Janet listened intently to the projected rambling thoughts of a longtime acquaintance. This marked the fifth instance within the previous three months that Janet had been awakened by the thoughts of Brittany, with each of those projections becoming progressively clearer. As a byproduct of the episodes, Janet had become aware of multiple feelings, opinions, emotions, and actions that the younger woman had probably intended to remain as privileged information. That belief was painfully solidified for Janet, as the most recent of Brittany's projections, which had to have been accidental in nature, openly revealed a deceitful plan specifically targeted toward her. With that projection Janet suddenly realized that Brittany wasn't the sweet and simple minded hormonal young woman that she had often pretended to be, and had done a masterful job of fooling those around her, including Janet and Aurora, into a few false assumptions.

In Janet's case, one such assumption unfortunately involved Colt. Until now, Janet had believed that the younger woman had desires of seducing Colt for as long as it took until he succumbed to her obvious and more youthful temptations. Additionally, she had developed the thought that Colt harbored secret desires for Brittany after the young tart blindsided him with a passionate kiss. Brittany's projections had now proved that the first of those assumptions was completely false, and with Colt's subsequent death, the second, true or not, was of little consequence. Although upset with Brittany for the various levels of deceit that she had perpetrated upon Ross and the recruits, Janet was really angry that Brittany had been able to play her into behaving like a foolish adolescent school girl.

While staring at the ceiling to digest all that had been heard throughout the series of Brittany's projections, Janet pondered over the joy she would feel by slapping the vicious woman in the face for her actions. Then for the first time she seriously considered the possibility of what Hank had proposed when the alien telepathically informed her he was in route to Earth. Now, as with Hank, Janet became a believer that their alien friend had received her thought projected plea for assistance with the virus. The idea had become more plausible to her now that Brittany had obviously developed the same telepathic ability.

The next morning at breakfast, Janet attempted to pull Hank's attention away from the now nearly always present engineering schematics or drawings. She asked, "Hank, can I talk to you for a minute?"

Without looking up from the set of drawings that held his attention, he replied, "Sure mom. What's on your mind?"

"Well for one thing, I would like you to look at me when I'm talking to you."

Realizing he had been rude, Hank looked up and said, "Sorry about that mom. What do you want to talk about?"

"I hadn't mentioned this to you after any of the other occasions, but I feel you should know about it now."

"Alright mom, go ahead."

"Last night I heard another vivid telepathic projection, but the thoughts didn't come from our alien friend."

"Then who did they come from?"

"Her name is Brittany. She is one of the recruits."

"That's interesting!"

"Do you remember her?"

"Sure I remember her, and I also remember that you and Aurora didn't like her very much."

"It's not that I didn't like her. We had known each other during our time in captivity, and I even considered her to be a friend. What's probably more accurate is that I was afraid of her and what she represented. Aurora felt the same way, and I can understand how when you were only eight you would have interpreted our behavior as not liking her."

"Alright, so why were you afraid of her then?"

"Aurora and I both thought that Brittany was trying to steal away Tikal or your father, but now I know that's wasn't true."

"And you know that how?"

"I know that because of the content of her telepathy last night, and that's why I wanted to talk to you. I thought about it for quite some time while lying awake, and I think you were correct when you first suggested that I had projected thoughts to our alien friend."

"That was a couple of years ago mom, but I'm glad to know that you think I was right."

"I do, and Brittany has provided the evidence to back it up. If she can telepathically project, then it makes sense that I possibly could too."

"I agree, and we have known for a long time that she has the ability to receive."

"That's true, each of the long term abductees can."

"So have you attempted to contact Brittany, or for that manner, any of the three pilots?"

"No I haven't. I may try to contact the pilots, but I'm not sure yet if I want to contact Brittany."

"But you freely admit that you once considered her to be a friend."

"True."

"And then more recently, you were only afraid of her somehow stealing dad away from you."

"True."

"Well obviously that isn't an issue anymore, so why not make an attempt at contacting an old friend telepathically?"

"Because now, based on what I have heard from her own telepathy, I don't like her very much!"

CHAPTER TWENTY-FOUR
REACHING OUT

Although she had remained silent toward Brittany with her own projections, Janet continued to receive, with increased frequency, the unintended telepathy from Katoomba. Each of Brittany's thought projections seemed to have added strength and clarity, so Janet took that as a sign. She theorized that it had to be only a matter of time before Brittany would stumble upon the reality of her own telepathic abilities.

What had been a pleasant development and surprise was the recent presence of a second telepathic voice from Katoomba. Although Janet was willing to attempt contact with the man, she was cautious as to the possibility of Brittany also receiving their exchange of thoughts. She decided to take an appropriate precaution by first projecting a short message toward her alien friend inquiring how she should proceed. The response was quick, "Telepathy begins with internal focus. When you intend to telepathically communicate with a single entity as opposed to many, then you must focus only on that entity and the message that you wish to project."

That seemed logical, so armed with that knowledge; Janet found a quiet place and focused solely on her intended target in Katoomba. Her first projected message was simple, "Hello Joseph, this is Janet from Dripping Springs. Please don't be afraid, but there is evidence to prove that you have recently developed telepathic abilities just like me."

While gazing eastward toward the ruins of Sydney, Joseph suddenly placed both hands on his head and closed his eyes tightly. When Adelaide asked, "What's wrong Joseph? Do you feel sick?"

"No, I feel fantastic. It would be difficult to explain, but the strangest sensation just came over me."

Before having the opportunity to attempt any further explanation, Janet's projected thoughts could be heard again. "Please don't let Brittany know that you can hear me, as I will make contact with her separately."

He didn't know why such a request had come across, but Joseph knew that Adelaide and Brittany were best friends. They told each other seemingly everything, and as a former military pilot he understood the need for privileged information upon occasion. Turning to Adelaide, he created a cover by saying, "It's no big deal honey. I just have a slight headache."

The third telepathic message then came to him, and Joseph needed to exhibit a stern poker face while absorbing all that it entailed. He had heard, "I know that you can receive my telepathy Joseph, and I have heard your unintentional thought projections from time to time as well. Our alien friends have been most helpful in the enhancement of my telepathic ability, and now I can help you do the same. Please start by focusing only on me, and then try to project a simple message."

A moment later, Janet smiled broadly as she received a humorous message of, "Is this working Janet? If so, then I hope I'm not screaming at you."

Her immediate response was, "Yes it's working. I can hear you Joseph, and the volume level is fine. If you are not alone, then please focus on me again when you are."

When five minutes had elapsed without receiving any projection, Janet moved on to other things. Realizing that she had effectively planted the telepathic seed within Joseph, she knew that he would contact her when he had the opportunity to do so privately.

When Joseph did contact Janet several hours later, his telepathy contained a simple greeting. After responding, she then received a series of completely understandable questions. As anticipated, Joseph inquired, "How did you discover that you had this ability? When did you first develop it? And is there anyone other than the two of us who can also use telepathy?"

In fielding those questions, and others that followed, Janet realized that she should attempt to make contact with the other two long term abductees who had returned to Earth as recruits. Then she reiterated to Joseph, "I would appreciate it if you could keep the knowledge of our telepathic abilities away from Brittany for the time being."

"Sure Janet. I'll do that, but can you tell me why?"

"You may know her quite differently as you have spent several years in the same population center with her, but her thought projections have revealed deceit in the past. The global population is already frustrated with each of us living well beyond others with the virus, so we don't need to add fuel to the fire. As we further develop our abilities we should proceed with caution, and I'm just not sure that Brittany can be discreet with the knowledge, or use, of telepathic communication."

"I understand your concern Janet, as she and my wife tend to talk about everything. You can rest easy though, I won't tell either of them anything about this."

"Thanks Joseph. Let's communicate again soon."

Following that communication, Janet contacted, and then responded to, the initial questions of the other two pilots. She was pleased to have introduced the concept of their telepathic abilities to each of the three men, and that they had accepted their personal evolution shift in stride.

Although all four members of their select group had been able to receive alien telepathy for many years, Janet was proud of knowing that she helped to establish a never before accomplished link. Now those same individuals could employ telepathy, both the projecting and receiving of, with the alien species and each other. Adding to that fascinating new reality was the fact that the communication between each of the humans could be accomplished from locations separated by thousands of miles. Janet believed that each member would need to be discreet with regard to who they informed of their collective ability for the time being, and politely asked them to do so. She also felt it was just as important to continue their personal development, but that could only be accomplished through determined focus and practice. Understanding that, she also suggested that they attempt discussions with each other, and as a group, on a regular basis.

CHAPTER TWENTY-FIVE
SILENT CONVERSATION

Having entered system ₹-829, the newly designed fast alien scout ship prepared for arrival on the blue multi-ringed third planet. The flight log would reveal that the voyage had established a new record pace for traversing that portion of the quadrant, but that was not the pilot's immediate concern. Full breaking then brought the vessel into what, at least in a visual sense, appeared to be a virtual crawl.

The maneuver commenced while at an equal distance from the host star with the fifth, and largest, of the eight planet system. Then the adjustable viewing screen revealed a familiar sight, as the multi-colored gas giant, with dozens of orbiting moons, was clearly visible in its granger. The magnificent view was brief however, as the floating marbles quickly shrank from sight.

After adjusting and locking the optics of the view screen to a forward facing perspective, the much smaller mass of the red fourth planet appeared within minutes. Then just seconds after leaving that orb in their wake, an unknown object was detected on a proximity monitor. Fearing that they may have miscalculated a comets path or had encountered a rogue asteroid, the pilot prepared for evasive maneuvers. Then the view screen revealed a small slow moving metallic object with a strange shinning flat surface protruding from it. Neither he nor his two crewmates had ever seen such a bizarre configuration for any type of space vehicle in any of the known systems, and were therefore understandably curious.

Mimicking a physical movement of Ross and many other humans, the pilot shrugged his small shoulders and thought projected, "The Earthlings must have developed a new design for the probes that they send to their neighboring planets."

Nodding with comprehension, his navigator replied, "Do you think it's a propulsion system of some kind?"

"That would seem logical, but we can't be sure."

"Should I plot a course around it to investigate?"

"No. We need to get to that blue planet now coming into view as quickly as possible. Besides, if that is some new propulsion system, we don't know if our circling to investigate would somehow affect it or the surrounding vacuum."

As the scout ship entered orbit for final slowing, and then proceeded to the chosen landing site near Janet's location, the alien pilot smiled inwardly. He couldn't wait to discuss at length when, and how, Janet had put the pieces together. Not long after his initial response to her plea, and the scout ships subsequent hurried departure, the alien had received another brief telepathic message from her. That message had become the next logical step within her shifted evolution, and revealed the new level of illumination that was beginning to transpire within Janet's mind. She had projected, "If this entire episode hasn't been a dream or some weird hallucination, then I truly believe that you can hear my thoughts. If my assessment is accurate, then would you please respond?"

Later that day a bolt of telepathic projection nearly knocked her off her feet, as she heard the reply of, "Yes, I can hear you Janet. Are you still in need of assistance?"

After her reply of "Yes, most definitely", it would be sometime before the alien received another message from her. He was prepared for that based on something that his father had confided in him long ago. Some species, without realizing it, had difficulty accepting the wonders of their evolutionary process, and had limited themselves because of it. Although the ability for telepathic communication wasn't present within the majority of their cataloged species, civilizations containing the correct building blocks to do so had occasionally delayed advancement for centuries of their respective timelines as a result of pre-programed beliefs. They had effectively discarded the notion that their species was capable of telepathy.

Based on her next communication, the alien believed that Janet had required an Earth year or perhaps longer to fully digest the prospect that she was now capable of telepathic thought. At that time Janet had asked quite plainly, "It's obvious that I'm still in the infant stage of knowing how to properly use this new telepathic ability of mine, so I'm not sure if any of my messages get through to you until you respond. Can you tell me how many others of my species, on this planet or other worlds, have developed the same capability?"

Janet's inquiry had revealed humbleness not often displayed when one discovers they have a profound new ability at their disposal, and had once again demonstrated Janet's progression of self-awareness and enlightenment. Pleased by those early signs of acceptance toward her evolutionary shift, the alien responded in kind. "Thank you Janet. You have asked an important question while accepting a limitation. You, and those of your species, will need to ponder both aspects of your inquiry as you attempt to move into a new evolutionary era. I know that others of your species have developed a telepathic ability, but you are the first to communicate with me. Soon others, possibly without realizing it, will join you. Your role is to be patient, and help them along the path."

That projection exchange had taken place only a few days prior by the alien timeline, but it had been more than two Earth years into the past. Since that time there had been less than a human handful of thought exchanges, but each had showed promise with regard to Janet's early development. They also possessed a common thread, the need for help.

As the scout ship moved into position for touchdown, a group of citizens from within the Dripping Springs collective gathered around. Their numbers were significantly diminished when compared to the day that Ross and his group of genetic recruits had been deposited, but from the view screen their welcoming demeanor appeared to be unchanged. Smiling faces and waves of their arms revealed their pleasure in the alien's return, and that became an instant comfort. Before opening the hatch for descent, the alien pilot projected, "Janet, are you there? Can you hear me?"

Within seconds he received a telepathic reply of, "Yes, I'm here. If you can hear me then you must be forewarned before you disembark. I'm glad you have arrived, and I know that you came as quickly as possible. Unfortunately there are some among us that don't feel the same way, as they believe that your species has ignored their needs."

"Ignored their needs? Perhaps those who feel that way misunderstood our intent. We never expected to return on a regular basis except for the potential of friendly visitation. Do any of those humans pose a threat to me or my crew?"

"No they don't, so it's safe for all of you to disembark. Those that I speak of are few in number, and just scared by our current predicament. Besides, you have already completed the journey to our doorstep, so why turn away now?"

"You make a good point Janet, and based on your level of concern over the problem at hand, it's understandable that some of your citizens are scared. If you say that it's safe for us to disembark, then we shall do so momentarily."

"Thank you. It has been nearly three Earth years since you heard my request for assistance, and we are now in more desperate need for it than we were at that time."

Shortly after their long awaited face to face reunion, and subsequent interactions with several other humans, the alien projected to Janet, "Can any of these people receive your telepathic communications?"

"A handful of these people might hear the occasional fragment, but there are three others who hear me clearly."

"Well, that's a beginning."

"Do you think that more will eventually hear me?"

"Yes I do Janet. Although they may never develop the ability to project as you have, some will eventually be able to at least receive."

"That's a lot to absorb. Do you really believe that I'm capable of communicating with the masses non-verbally?"

"Yes I do, but those you intend to share telepathy with would need to develop the skill of reception first. Remember, each of you who had been long term abductees were kept in part because of your ability to receive telepathic projections, but only a minor percentage of humans, including those who relocated with you to ₹-593-ℜπ-2-2, have developed that skill. What I want to know is, since learning of your ability, have you discovered any others who can project as you do?"

"Well I'm certain that there are at least four other people on this planet that can project telepathically, but I don't believe that the one female is aware of her ability yet."

"That's interesting, have you contacted her?"

"No I haven't, because I don't want her to know that I can hear her."

"That's a strange reaction to learning of another who shares your telepathic abilities. I have never encountered that thought process with any other developed species, so you may be unique in that regard. Could you explain why you believe that she is not yet aware of her ability?"

"Mainly because her thoughts are mostly unfiltered, and they seem to be jumbled with no real structure to them. Don't misunderstand me, she's intelligent beyond what most people, including myself, had perceived her to be, and can develop a plan of action to suit her needs quickly. I didn't know about one such plan until I began to receive her thoughts on a regular basis, but she had used her craftiness to deceive me in the past. Unfortunately for her, the memory thoughts of that event have blown her cover."

"Blown her cover? What does that mean?"

"It's an old Earth expression. Basically it means that a person has pretended to be something that they aren't, and that they have been discovered to be false. In this case I now understand Brittany for the person that she truly is as opposed to the artificial one that I believed her to be, and she won't be able to fool me any longer."

"So that's why you don't want to answer her?"

"That's right. I want to gather more information about any of her past, or future, plans before she realizes that I can hear her thoughts. Besides, I can't respond to her thoughts if she doesn't ask me a question!"

"I now understand your feelings toward her, but you need to be careful."

"What do you mean?"

"You are doing very well with your projected telepathy considering the brief amount of time that you have possessed the ability, and you should be proud of that accomplishment and the evolutionary shift that it represents. I will caution you though; you are playing a dangerous game."

"Why do you say that?"

"Brittany may be able to receive your projections as clearly as you can hear hers, and you should be mindful of that. You just admitted that she is capable of deceiving you, and if she is listening to your thoughts, or the others that you speak of, then she could attempt to do so again."

Having somehow been neglectful of that rather logical possibility, Janet took a moment to reflect on what she may have inadvertently revealed during telepathy with any of the three pilots. Then she said verbally, "Thank you my friend, you have given me some good advice. I will be careful, as I'm sure that my skill level is weak. I will need much more practice in the refinement of both my receiving and projecting abilities."

With a positive nod, the alien then projected, "It has been our experience that every form of life, no matter what system they reside within, needs practice when they first develop a telepathic ability. It's refreshing for me to exchange thought projections with a member of a species who will freely admit that they have a potential shortcoming, but why do you believe that your skill level is weak?"

"I'm not yet proficient with my telepathic ability. When I communicate with you, or others of your species, I can hear those projections with total clarity regardless of the distance between us. In my case however, I feel that the range must be limited and can be sporadic. My projections are not always properly received, and I will need improvement to ensure that my thoughts are only projected at those that I wish to hear them. I believe that you can help me with that problem, and I hope that you are willing to become my instructor."

"Try not to underestimate your potential Janet. My clarity, as you like to call it, is shared by all of my species. We have employed telepathic communication for several hundred thousand of your Earth years, so for us the process has become extremely fine-tuned. In contrast, you, and others of your species like you, are at the dawn of a new revelation. Therefore it's completely understandable that you have not yet realized how to either control your ability, or fully harness it. I will help you with that process if that is what you truly desire, but first I would like to know how you became aware that your projection range is limited or sporadic."

"That's easy. You wouldn't have ignored my projections during the past few years if you had received them."

"That's true."

"Then it's logical to assume that you didn't respond because of my limitations. I obviously didn't project each of them with equal strength."

CHAPTER TWENTY-SIX

TAKING CHARGE

Seated with the new administrator who had recently assumed a position that Tori occupied before her death, Janet realized that the young man was perhaps more ill-equipped than the one who had been her initial replacement. It wasn't his fault really. He, like the administrator before him, was well shy of turning thirty when given the responsibility of tending to the many needs of Dripping Springs. Each had been thrust into a role of leadership that neither had been properly prepared for, and unfortunately for them, their performance magnified the competency that had been displayed by Tori while tending to the task before them.

Although Janet had maintained her anger with Tori for years due to her being the mother for one of Colt's children, perhaps it was time to move on. Hindsight had showed her that the anger was unjust. Those physical implications associated with the gene enrichment program had absolutely no bearing on Tori's ability and skill as a former administrator.

Leaning toward the young man, Janet whispered, "Do you think that we should make this gathering an open forum?"

"What do you mean?"

With sarcasm in her tone, she said, "Should we allow those present to freely ask questions of our alien friends?"

"I don't know Janet. Do you think that's a good idea?"

Janet thought, well at least this one is willing to seek out opinions. Then more sympathetically, she replied, "Yes I do. Please don't exclude their voice from this discussion."

"Alright, how should we go about that?"

His question brought forth a new thought of, one step forward and one step back. Then she smiled at the young man and said, "If you will allow me, I'll take care of it."

"Thanks for the help Janet. I'm not really sure what to do in situations like this one."

Placing an index finger over her lips to quiet the man, she then leaned closer and whispered, "It's certainly a positive sign of your leadership ability to admit when you may have a shortcoming, but as someone who is new to the job, you invite danger by doing so verbally while in public."

Then nodding positively, he whispered back, "Thanks Janet. I think I understand what you mean."

After patting his knee, Janet stood up and said, "If we can all remain somewhat orderly, then this will be an open forum. When we call on you, please feel free to ask our alien friends any questions that you might have. As you already know, he can only respond telepathically. A few of you might be able to hear his thoughts if you concentrate, but if not, then I can translate for you if you wish."

The first question proposed to the aliens was actually more of a statement, and although the content was totally predictable, it still made Janet feel rather uneasy. The man of early to mid-thirties who was obviously in the late stages of infection said, "Since you brought the small contingent of humans back here nearly seven Earth years ago, this planet has been facing a problem of epic proportions. In spite of our supposed best efforts to discover a cure for the affliction that has now caused several thousands of deaths, or even a way to prevent further contamination, our medical community is at a self-admitted loss. Within each of our few global communities the population has been severely depleted, and the damage to our genetic makeup has been tremendous. If this virus that has attacked us continues on its current path for much longer, we will not be able to recover from it."

Having listened carefully, Janet said, "As a member of that global medical team who has been unable to assist the population, I can only say that I'm sorry for our shortcomings. Now, do you have a question for our alien friends?"

"Yes I do, and it's probably the same question that everyone else has. What can he do to help us find a cure?"

Janet knew that the man was right. His question would be one of the few that would be on the mind of everyone. That and, why did the aliens bring infected humans back to a harmonious world? In truth, she was also curious to hear the answers to both questions. If the thought had been to salvage the dying gene pool of the planet, then why insert a group who could potentially contaminate all those who were still alive? While pondering that thought for a moment, Janet felt her knees buckle and she nearly missed her seat on the way toward the floor. What she had heard via the thought projection of the alien as he answered the first question astonished her, and it became evident that she was not the only one in the small collective to receive his response.

One of those who had been able to receive alien telepathy for years was Kristyn, and although Janet had not noticed when she joined the assembled crowd, her presence suddenly became abundantly clear. While attempting to steady herself, Janet heard Kristyn loudly exclaim, "I can't believe it! What do you mean you won't be able to help us?

Her question understandably created a reaction among all those present, and growing murmurs of negativity were quickly heard. For a brief moment Janet was concerned that her promise of safety to her old friend and his crew had been premature, but no move was made toward any of the three aliens. Then she witnessed a delightful surprise, as the new administrator stood up and took a stance. While motioning with his arms for quiet, he said, "Now come on everyone, just relax for a minute. Let's get some clarification as to the alien's response before things get out of control."

Again Kristyn rang out with conviction, "We don't need clarification to his response. I know what I heard."

Janet stood again, and then focused while projecting her thoughts toward the brave young lady. The message was direct, and carried significant weight. "Kristyn, this is Janet. If you can hear my thoughts as you have just heard our alien friend, then please keep calm and don't yell out. For now, it would be better if you just gave me a signal of understanding. Could you please scratch the top of your head for me?"

For several seconds Kristyn stared at Janet with a high level of astonishment. While contemplating how to respond to the magnitude of the moment, she experienced a flashback. During recent months there had been several instances when she thought she had heard Janet's voice for a few words or a short phrase, but there was never any sight of her when it happened. On each of those occasions Kristyn's belief was that her imagination was simply running wild, but she suddenly felt differently about that theory. Was it really possible? Did Janet, or other humans, possess the ability to communicate via telepathic thought projection? With those questions swirling about in her brain, Kristyn raised a hand toward the crown of her head and complied with Janet's telepathic request.

With the signal delivered, Janet realized that the entire message must have gotten through. That could probably be attributed to the close proximity of Kristyn, or perhaps it was due to her current determined focus. That was insignificant at the moment, and could be experimented with and determined at a later time. What was significant was that her telepathy could be received by yet another of her species, and this one, like the three pilots, was most definitely a friend. After a brief smile, Janet decided to press the issue and project again. Her message was, "Thank you Kristyn. It's good to know that you can hear my thoughts, as you are one of very few that can. I have recently developed this telepathic ability, and have very little, if any, control over how to properly use it. Now could you please tug on your ear if I'm still coming through?"

In an instant Kristyn did as she was asked, and a few seconds later gulped when a third telepathic request came her way. That message stated, "Now please keep calm about what our alien friend has said. I'm sure that there's an explanation, and he has always been forthcoming with information."

At that moment they both heard the voice of the alien, as he projected, "That's very good projection Janet, and Kristyn, thanks for listening to her thoughts. I'm only projecting toward the two of you right now, but Janet is correct. In a moment I will send out a telepathic explanation to all those present who can receive it, but I wanted to communicate with the two of you first. Kristyn, please do that thing again with your ear if you understand that I can, and will, help your species, but not in exactly the same way that was just asked of me."

After a nod and a tug of her right ear, she heard, "Good, now remain calm as I respond to the question at hand."

Then Janet projected toward her, "I'm sure everything will be fine Kristyn, and we can talk about all of this later."

Their alien friend added, "I would like to communicate with both of you, and Hank, in a more private setting when we have time. As you are now aware, there is a most important topic to discuss and I feel that Hank would also benefit from being part of that conversation."

CHAPTER TWENTY-SEVEN
EXPANDING THE CIRCLE

Throughout the next year, Janet, with the guidance of her alien friend, continued to develop her telepathic abilities. Early on within that process, she worked extensively with both Kristyn and Hank as a result of their private discussion with the alien. During that conversation, it had been disclosed that both of the youngsters could, with determined focus and practice, expand upon the breakthrough that Janet and very few others had achieved. Although they were left in the dark as to how, their alien friend had informed them that they both possessed the untapped telepathic ability within. They were taught that as Janet became more proficient with her intended projections, she could help them learn how to develop and hone the same skill. In time, perhaps they could become tutors themselves.

As that year neared its conclusion, Janet realized that she had been woefully neglectful of her previous obligations. She became so involved with her own development and the subsequent tutelage of telepathic projection, that she had spent very little time working on a cure or preventative measure for the virus. In the course of that neglect, Janet had been unaware that the eighth year of her current residence on Earth had seen the virus gain momentum while relentlessly slashing its way on through the surviving population.

Always searching for a means to provide Kristyn with additional telepathic practice, Janet projected, "Has there been any recent updates that you're aware of with regard to the spreading of the virus?"

A moment later she heard, "Sure Janet, you know that we get them all the time at the communication center."

"That's good projection Kristyn; you're coming through very clearly. I'm almost afraid to ask, but are the reports from the other population centers still filled with negativity?"

"Yes they are, but perhaps we should meet privately in a few hours to discuss them. I'm currently training a few people on the correct use of the global communication system, and I don't want them to think that I have become disinterested or distracted while I'm focusing on telepathy with you."

Janet understood that Kristyn was only attempting to maintain their secrecy, so her response was quick. "I'll see you later then."

As the two ladies took a stroll on the beach, Hank kept an eye on Kristyn's three younger siblings. They enjoyed the SSP, and Hank liked to pedal them around various areas of the community. He had also developed a little math game that they enjoyed playing during such rides, so keeping them all occupied was less taxing than what others might have believed.

Kristyn reported the sad news to Janet that those who were infected now included several teenagers globally, and in some population centers they were as young as fifteen. Within Dripping Springs there were a handful of such cases, and two of them were people that Kristyn and Hank had come to know as friends. With the exception of the mysteriously blessed twenty-one Mayans, no one over twenty was clean of the virus any longer.

The news of the latest case being a young man of fifteen from Rio Paulo instantly made Janet nervous, as Hank was now sixteen. She also noticed the obvious look of concern on the face of Kristyn, now fifteen, and there was good reason. The young girl had vowed to Natiya during her final hours that she would do her absolute best to keep her younger siblings safe, and for two years she had done a splendid job of doing that. The harsh realization was that when Kristyn inevitably became infected, her promise would be more difficult to fulfill.

Janet sighed deeply when she realized the logic behind Kristyn's non-verbal belief. It was correct for Kristyn to assume that she, and Hank, would eventually test positive for the virus. Anyone would be rightfully scared to learn of that, and it made Janet realize that she hadn't been tested for quite some time. Although the progression of the virus had slowed within her system several years prior, it would still be prudent for her to receive an updated status of her infection level. With that she returned to the medical labs, and had one of the technicians draw a sample of her blood.

While waiting the ten minutes needed for her blood to be scanned and compared to previous results, Janet sat in quiet contemplation. What came from that was her feeling that if there were any comfort that could be derived from the newly reported information; it was that certain aspects of the virus had remained unchanged. Of specific note was the gestation period. From the earliest signs of infection on through to the subsequent throws of death, the duration was still determined in large part by the age of the victim. In simple terms, the younger the infected, the longer it took for the virus to completely overtake their system.

The loud voice of the lab technician then startled Janet back into the reality of the present moment, as he shouted, "I can't believe it, but I ran the test twice to be sure!"

Looking up Janet replied, "Why? What did you find?"

"The progression of the virus within your system has somehow completely halted. There is no measurable difference between your test results of today, and those that you took six months ago."

Janet stared at the young technician for a moment, and then replied, "If this is a joke, I'm not laughing!"

"I have known you for a couple of years Janet, and I wouldn't joke about such a thing. I'm telling you there has been no advancement during the past six months."

Realizing the sincerity of the man, she replied, "Well then, that's great news. Now what do we do about it?"

"Well, we know that the Mayan blood samples which have been tested repeatedly for possible prevention or a cure have yielded no results, but yours might."

A new revelation struck Janet, as it dawned on her that she would become a giant pin cushion as each of the Mayans had been if the news got out. She remembered that a few years back Tikal showed noticeable irritation throughout that entire process, and Janet felt confident that she would exhibit similar feelings under those conditions. With that thought she said, "Would you mind if we kept the results of my tests quiet for a couple of hours? I need to take care of a few things before becoming the next circus attraction."

"I don't know what a circus attraction is, but as a favor to the lady who taught me most of what I know about the medical labs, I'll keep quiet about this for a little while."

"Thanks, I'll be back later."

With that Janet retreated and then focused hard on projecting to her alien friend and the three pilots. Her thoughts revealed a concise message of, "I have just received the results from my recent blood test, and there has been an alarming discovery. Please find someone in your respective medical labs that you trust to keep quiet about the results, and get a fresh blood test. If my theory is correct, then your results will be alarming as well. Thanks for doing this and contact me when you can."

A few hours later the first of the telepathy came to her, and it didn't take long for the others to follow. Joseph, and one other pilot, had received results to coincide with Janet's. Each of the three had just become, for the second time, dramatic exceptions to the well-established rules of the global virus. Sadly the last, and youngest, of the pilots, had not received the same news with his test results. The virus had slowed further toward stagnation, but it was still advancing within him.

Meanwhile the alien listened with great interest to their collective telepathy, and fielded questions or commented upon the theories that they each presented. He also pondered over the implication of how some had become virally stagnant, and how long, without providing the answers they sought, that it would take them to put more of the pieces together.

CHAPTER TWENTY-EIGHT

MAGNIFICENT QUANDARY

Standing on the beach beside her alien friend during another beautiful sunset, Janet projected, "You and your crew have been with us for an entire Earth year now, and I'm so grateful for everything that each of you has taught us."

"Thank you Janet. I wish that it was possible for us to stay longer, as your species continues to astonish those of mine with your inquisitive nature and steadfast determination."

"Wish you could stay? You're not leaving are you?"

"Yes we are Janet. When your host star that is now fading from view returns in several of your Earth hours to rise over this community, then we will depart for our home world."

"But when you first arrived, you claimed that you not only could, but that you would, help our species."

"That's true, and I have."

"But you haven't helped us defeat the virus!"

"I'm aware of that Janet, but I never claimed that I could, or would, help you defeat the virus. I informed you that my help would come, but not in a form exactly the way it had been asked of me."

"But I don't understand!"

"Yes you do Janet. You understand much more than you think you do. The assistance of my species toward yours has come in many ways, and you are aware of that. Soon you will discover additional wisdom. All you need is a little time to think about the situation from a non-emotional perspective, and that contemplation will lead you in the right direction."

"Lead me in the right direction to what?"

"Well, to the answers that you currently seek from me of course. You are a perceptive member of your species who was chosen by our species many of your Earth centuries ago. It was speculated then that you were a prodigy, and one of only a few hundred of your species who could perhaps be capable of shaping the next evolutionary shift."

"Shape an evolutionary shift in my species? I think that you must have the wrong girl. I would have no idea how I'm supposed to accomplish something of that magnitude!"

"Stay focused Janet. Our assessment has already been proven to be correct, as one aspect of that shift is based on what you're doing with me at this very moment."

"You mean two-way telepathic communication?"

"Yes, but it goes beyond that. You, and a few others, have initiated the process without realizing it. Now continue by asking the right questions within yourself, and if you do, the answers will come your way eventually. When that happens, and it will happen, you will briefly think of yourself as a fool for not seeing it more clearly from the start."

"So I, or the others like me, need to dig deeper for the truly important questions and answers to our future."

"Not necessarily Janet. Sometimes digging deeper can only get you stuck in the hole. When you ask the questions, think of the reasons or answers that might be more obvious."

"That sounds like the type of philosophical conversation that Ross would have enjoyed."

"He did Janet. Ross and I discussed it several times."

With a smile on her face, Janet then asked, "Is there any more information that you could give me right now?"

Ross once told me of a human phrase that might be applicable in this instance. He had said to me, "I can't spell out everything for you, as that would limit your development."

"Yes, Ross would have said something like that. But don't you think that something as important as a shift in human evolution would create an exception to that belief?"

"I see your point Janet, so I will provide you with one more clue. Your species advancement, along with your own, hinges upon the combined efforts aimed at the greater good. As very few of you are currently capable of projection, your species can't afford to selectively silence a single voice. You must include Brittany when you and the others participate in either individual or group telepathy. Her powers are ready to blossom, and it's insignificant how you feel towards her personally, she will require your guidance to properly unleash her new found ability."

With that the alien moved away to begin preparations for his departure from Earth, while Janet was left to ponder all that had been projected between them. She remained on the beach for another hour, and gazed upon the heavens as the countless stars continued to appear in the increasing darkness. Glancing at the faint star that held their former home moon captive within its gravitational grip, Janet whispered aloud, "I hope that Jessica, the colony, and our Mayan friends, are all doing better than we are."

The following morning, not long after the first hint of daylight, Janet received a telepathic projection from Hank. The message jolted her into action, as she heard, "Hey mom, the sun will be up soon. You need to wake up and get ready right now if you want to see our old friend before he leaves."

Springing to her feet with fear that she may already be too late, Janet projected, "Don't wait for me Hank. You go ahead, and make sure they don't leave before I get there!"

"Alright mom, but how long will you be?"

"Just a couple of minutes, I promise."

Then jogging up toward the alien vessel, Janet noticed that there were far less people to bid them farewell than there had been to welcome them the previous year. Spotting Hank and Kristyn bracketing her three siblings, she projected, "Have you two seen or heard anything from the aliens?"

Without turning Hank projected, "Not yet, but they have initiated their propulsion system. You better hurry up and get here mom, they could leave any minute."

Then all five of them heard a verbal reply from not far behind them, "I'm here. Thanks for saving me a place."

Surveying their immediate surroundings and locating plentiful open ground, Hank playfully replied, "Your welcome. As you can plainly see, we had to hold off several people in order to secure a place for you."

Janet moved the final few feet to stand next to Hank, and then after lightly punching his arm sarcastically replied, "Every day you remind me more and more of your father and Ross with that dry wit of yours, and that's not necessarily a good thing."

Before Hank could reply, the hatch of the alien scout ship hissed open. Standing in the doorway were the three alien visitors, and they each offered up a gesture of farewell with a slight wave of a four long fingered hand. Then Janet realized that she would not be afforded the opportunity for a face to face goodbye, as the hatch began to close again. She quickly projected, "It has been wonderful having you here for the past year while teaching us so much. I hope to see you again soon."

Each returned a short telepathic reply of thanks and goodwill, but the pilot added more. He projected, "You must remain focused Janet. Think about why certain things are the way they are, while others are not. If and when you develop an answer to that all-encompassing question, then you can think about the impact that certain offspring might provide for the future. At that moment of answering that second question, you will know what needs to be done. You must trust in all those around you who can help bring your species destiny to fruition, and communicate with me again should you require additional assistance."

As the hatch hissed to a close, and the outline shape disappeared from view to signify a complete seal, Janet said aloud, "Well that's a big help!"

Seconds later those few that were assembled could feel the rush of air around them, but there was barely an audible sound to the lift-off. Moving with tremendous speed, the alien vessel shrank from their view and within the briefest of moments had escaped the confines of Earth's atmosphere.

CHAPTER TWENTY-NINE
LOCATING THE PIECES

As they approached the midway point of their return from system ₹-829 to the home world, the alien pilot received what he considered to be the inevitable telepathic projection from Janet. He calculated that during the brief amount of time that their fast scout ship had been traveling on its current trajectory, Earth, or ₹-829-ℑπ-3, had completed one and a half cycles around its host star. Based on the content of Janet's telepathy toward him, it was obvious that there had been several developments throughout that time which had enabled her to finally fit several pieces of the puzzle together.

Janet's message began with news that within a few weeks of the alien departure, she began to communicate with Brittany telepathically. Not long after the initial shock within Brittany had worn off, the three pilots helped smooth her transition and education by participating in individual or group thought exchanges. Since that time Brittany had exhibited a surprising amount of progress with regard to her skill, and the restraint that was necessary in order to maintain a level of secrecy about her telepathic ability.

Throughout that process she and Joseph had spent an inordinate amount of time with each other as she learned to refine her skills, and that was logical as they both lived in the same community. Unfortunately, the innocent mentoring relationship with Brittany that Joseph had developed was not viewed by Adelaide with similar enthusiasm. She was nearing her final days of life when her husband and Brittany began spending so much extra time together, and in her hallucination phase, Adelaide had become consumed with jealous rage over her interpretation of Brittany's long term intentions. Janet would have actually found mild amusement in the situation if the entire episode hadn't been so tragic. Brittany had somehow managed to lure yet another woman, on her deathbed no less, into forfeiting what remained of her self-control, and she had done so while being completely innocent.

In the wake of all that was transpiring in Katoomba, Janet had also been hearing several fragmented thoughts for several weeks in a language that was foreign to her. Aided by the translation skills that Kristyn had developed while working in the communication center, they soon realized that the language was Mayan. What Janet heard must have been the thoughts of Tikal, and any of the other twenty Mayan recruits scattered about the planet. Even though Tikal had become well versed in the language of his deceased wife Aurora, his unintended telepathic thoughts had projected in his native tongue. It was therefore a reasonable assumption that the same could be said for the other Mayans, so Kristyn began formalizing a plan. When the time was right, she, with Tikal's help, would inform them of their ability.

A few months later the last of the three pilots had joined Janet and his flying brethren with test results that revealed a complete stagnation of the virus within his system. The same could not yet be said of Brittany, but she was the youngest of the five long term abductees. Janet and the others were confident that Brittany would eventually receive the same test results, but would there be anyone other than the five of them and the Mayans still alive to embrace the news?

That question had been broached only because the age of those infected continued to drop slightly. The youngest case now stood at eleven, and the girl in what had been Japan had tested negative only three months prior. With that news the local administrator in that population center, only twenty-five herself, initiated a plan to increase the frequency of testing. Her counterparts in each community quickly followed suit, and Janet crossed her fingers that both Hank and Kristyn would remain negative. A week later when each of their respective results eased her worried mind, she experienced the mixed feelings of joy and confusion.

While at a temporary loss of understanding, Janet sat and pondered why some boys around the planet aged twelve, thirteen, and even a couple that were fourteen, had tested negative. Conversely, there were just as many younger than Hank's current age of nearly eighteen that had also tested positive, but Hank had not. Kristyn had also been spared up to that point, and she recently turned seventeen, but there were many older than the eleven year old that were in the positive category. It just didn't make any sense as to why the bulk of the girls were testing positive at a younger age. Although it was true that in most cases girls began to behave like adults sooner than boys, they shouldn't be penalized by a horrific virus as a consequence of earlier maturity. Then the reason suddenly occurred to Janet why each sex had tested differently, and the reality of her discovery created momentary shame for not having realized it before.

She had informed the alien that her projection at that time to Kristyn had been, "I know that this may sound silly, but have you physically become a woman yet?"

Kristyn had then responded, "Well, good morning to you too Janet. I must admit, that's a strange question to begin a conversation with. But if you are referring to intimacy, then no, I have not yet become a woman."

Although Janet was the mother of three, and had been formally trained as a nurse before experiencing many years of service in the medical field, she was still embarrassed at needing to broach the subject. Kristyn showed all the physical characteristics of an adult woman, so the answer to her next question seemed to be rather obvious. Still, she needed to ask it, so Janet projected, "Kristyn, what about the physiological changes in your body?"

After a moment of silence that was probably due to utter shock, Janet heard, "I know that you have offered your help in whatever area that I might need Janet, but my mother and I had those discussions that involved my transition into womanhood many years ago."

"I figured as much Kristyn, and please believe that this topic is somewhat uncomfortable for me too, but has your transition occurred?"

Feeling annoyed by that question, Kristyn projected, "Yes it has, about four years ago if you must know. You should remember that you helped me when it began."

"That seems about the right time."

Still annoyed, she curtly projected, "Well I'm glad that you think so Janet, but why is this personal issue of mine important to you?"

"Sorry Kristyn, but I have a new theory about the virus. Unfortunately, you and Hank seem to be the only ones who could refute it."

"I see, so what's your theory Janet?"

"You have known that for years now we have been operating under the assumption that the virus strikes with a level of prejudice based on age, and there is plenty of data to substantiate that theory."

"Yes, I'm aware of that."

"Well, now I believe that the virus is striking the youth as each of them enters puberty. That could explain why so many of the girls are becoming infected before the boys."

Now far less annoyed after hearing the explanation of Janet's theory, Kristyn projected, "I see. Now I understand why you needed to ask me those intrusive questions, because I would appear to be an exception to your theory."

"You most certainly are, and so is Hank. Now we just need to figure out why."

The alien smiled inwardly as he listened to Janet's projected accounting of all that had transpired up to that point in time. He was then pleased to hear that she had at last come to the most logical of conclusions. Her projections revealed that throughout the next several Earth days the question that she and Kristyn had proposed became their central focus. They knew there had to be an answer, but what was it?

Janet had looked at the Mayan angle first. It had always been believed that an aspect of genetic code was responsible for their immunity to the virus, and that was why their blood had been so scrutinized in the past. If that belief were indeed true, then it still didn't explain the apparent immunity of Hank and Kristyn. A less likely cause would have been something in their diets, but Janet knew that investigating every possibility was necessary. Everyone here on new Earth consumed the same staples consisting of mainly large amounts of vegetables and fish, so that shouldn't create selected immunity. Janet then flashed back to the dietary practices on their former home moon. It was true that more meat was consumed by all of them during those years, and Janet remembered Colt teaming up with a Mayan hunting party in quest of the giant Wolf creatures or other wild game on several occasions. One such expedition had even taken place just days after Hank had been born and...

Suddenly the answer occurred to her, and Janet once again became ashamed for not having realized it sooner. That had to be the key. Janet had finally discovered the commonality that existed between the Mayans and Hank and Kristyn that explained their shared immunity. That answer didn't center on their respective lineage, it centered on where they had been born.

With a broad smile on her face, Janet projected to Kristyn, "I feel certain that I have just discovered the answer to our question!"

The return projection was immediate, "That's great news Janet. What did you discover?"

"Aside from the apparent immunity Kristyn, what do you and Hank have in common with the Mayans?"

After a long moment of silence, Janet then heard, "I give up. What do we all have in common?"

"It's the world where you were all born!"

CHAPTER THIRTY
PRESENTING THE SOLUTION

Janet's telepathic message then turned toward the actions of her species in the wake of the recent discovery, and she was proud to project that many had behaved admirably. Beyond Kristyn, the first to be informed was Hank, and he too felt a measure of shame for having overlooked the obvious commonality. Janet projected that their subsequent verbal discussion on the beach had led to an additional conclusion. The three of them believed it to be a logical assumption that their birth moon had also somehow enabled Hank, Kristyn, and the Mayans to possess the same telepathic ability as Janet and the other long term abductees. If that were true, and the alien was pleased that the humans had arrived at such a premise, then it was possible that many of those still living upon that second moon could possess the same untapped ability.

The next step had been to inform Tikal. As the most senior of the Mayan collective, their customs dictated that the others at least give him the respect of listening to what he had to say. He was not their King, nor did he ever claim the right to any special privileges, but he was the logical choice to spread the word among them. With Kristyn's help Tikal soon became more proficient with his projecting ability, and they provided a calming influence through the use of their joint telepathy. The task before them was significant, but Janet was confident that they could prepare the other Mayans for future events.

Now more than a year since that process had begun, Janet informed the alien that there were twenty-eight humans on Earth who could telepathically project. As had already been known, many others could receive, but none of them showed any sign of the potential to project as of this time. With the exception of Brittany, each of the aforementioned twenty-eight continued to exhibit either the immunity to, or a complete stagnation of, the virus within their systems. Her most recent blood test had confirmed further slowing of the progression, and it was believed that she would join their ranks soon.

Having brought the alien up to the current moment, Janet then projected, "If you have the time and desire to assist as you claim, then I would like to ask you a few questions."

Before agreeing to field any of her questions, the alien projected his thoughts of pleasure in Janet's development and leadership during an enlightening, yet challenging, transitional phase. Then he asked a series of questions, starting with, "Have you and Brittany resolved all of your differences?"

"Yes we have. She has matured significantly since we arrived back on Earth nearly ten years ago, and I realized that I may have been too harsh in my previous judgement of her."

"That's good to know Janet. Your realization will only assist with your own evolution and both of you have already become an important aspect of what is to come with regard to the evolution shift of your species."

"I don't understand. We have both become?"

"All of that will become clearer to you in the not too distant future, but for now, I have additional questions."

"Alright, go ahead."

"Now that you believe that the lower age limit of the viral infection has been determined, has your species collected data or run any tests to verify the theory?"

"Yes we have. There have been several more cases of young people entering puberty and almost immediately testing positive. We have also been closely monitoring those that we believe to be on the verge, and the tests remain negative until they begin their personal transition."

"So what does that tell you Janet?"

"Well, actually that leads to my first question of you."

"Go ahead."

"Although I believe that the young children will always be safe from infection, my concern is that none of them will ever be able to reach full adulthood."

"So what's your question?"

"Will every one of our children eventually become infected when then transition into young adulthood?"

"Yes they will."

"Then how can we possibly continue to repopulate our numbers? There can be no denying that Brittany and the ten Mayan women have done their part with regard to the gene enrichment program, but the females of our species are not capable of producing offspring forever!"

"That's correct Janet, and very few species are. So, what do you intend to do about that?"

"That's the problem. I don't know what to do!"

"There is a way that you can continue to repopulate your numbers, but it will not be easy. As you have discovered that the immunity to the virus belongs to those who were born on ₹-593-ᘘπ-2-2, you must now discover what has been the cause of the viral spread throughout all the adult members of your species."

"And how do you suggest that I proceed with that?"

"Stay focused Janet. Think of the possibilities."

A moment of contemplative silence followed before Janet resumed her projection of, "Well, because the immunity isn't genetically based, as had been originally believed to be true, then it would be reasonable for me to theorize that the spreading of the virus isn't based on human genetics either."

"That's correct."

"So perhaps it's something external."

"Yes, and?"

After another moment of silence, Janet projected, "Sorry, but it's just not coming to me."

"Try going back to the inception. The virus began with Ross on ₹-593-ȝπ-2-2, but it didn't become lethal and then spread to epidemic proportions until?"

"After you brought us back to..."

"Go ahead Janet. Complete the circle."

"Complete the circle? My God, is has something to do with Earth doesn't it?"

"Perhaps, now expand on that thought."

"Alright, so if it's not the food or water, maybe it's the air. That's it isn't it? The problem is atmospheric."

"Congratulations Janet, you have solved another piece to the puzzle."

"Thanks. I think!"

"We were as surprised by the problem as you are now. Throughout the centuries upon ₹-593-ȝπ-2-2, many of your species had innocently contracted the virus and spread it to others just as Ross did, but it was never fatal. Somehow when we returned your group to Earth, the natural atmospheric conditions of this planet altered the matrix of the virus."

"But if the cause of the continuing viral spread is somehow related to the atmosphere, then we are doomed!"

"We have encountered this problem before Janet, and the answer is still the same. You know more than you think you do. In fact, in this particular instance you know within your heart and soul what needs to be done. Just accept the truth, inform me that you understand the implications of that truth, and get on with the process of developing a plan!"

After a much longer than usual moment of silence, the navigator turned toward his commanding pilot and projected, "Do you really believe that she has the internal resolve to take the next step?"

"Yes. I do believe that Janet has the resolve within her, and she will take that next step. The thought of such an action had been entertained by her several times throughout the past few Earth years, but the fear of that reality kept her from broaching the subject with members of her species. I know Janet nearly as well as I knew her oldest offspring Ross, and a firm resolve for taking on extreme challenges is rooted within that family's genetic makeup. She will arrive at what is the logical conclusion for resolving the problem that they currently face, and then proceed with a plan of action to carry it out."

Their telepathic exchange was then interrupted when Janet chimed back in. As predicted, she had reached the logical conclusion of, "Alright, it's obvious that I can't deny the facts any longer. It certainly won't be the easiest of tasks for my species to prepare for, but we must all leave this planet if we hope to survive."

With a sigh of relief, her alien friend projected, "Thank you Janet for recognizing what is necessary and for taking a huge evolutionary step forward in the process. I'm sorry to inform you that it's the only way to halt further contamination of the virus. Your species must escape the natural atmospheric conditions that exist on your home planet, and if you can accomplish that most challenging task, then those of you who have not yet become infected will remain that way!"

"Alright, so we have lots of work to do then. Can you tell me how long that I have to prepare everyone before your transport vessels arrive?"

"I don't think you understand Janet."

"Sure I do. You need to take us all back to that pale green moon in system ₹-593."

"No. I'm sorry, but that won't be possible."

"What do you mean that won't be possible? Why not? You just informed me that all we needed to do was escape the natural atmospheric conditions of our home planet, and that would seem to be the most logical place for us to go. We can't get there on our own, so we need help from you."

"I know that you think so at the current moment, but returning to that moon is not the answer for you. Your current evolutionary shift on this planet is progressing at a different pace than those of your species on ₹-593-ठπ-2-2. Remember that most of this new Earth society as you like to call it had the benefit of twenty-six of your centuries after the apocalypse to evolve differently from a spiritual, philosophical, technological, and perhaps more importantly, a cooperative sense. Blending that mindset with members of your early twenty-first century society, or those that came before, wouldn't necessarily mix well. No Janet, we can't, and won't, return you to the moon they live upon. You must find another way."

After hearing that thought, Janet fell to the floor from the tremendous weight of what had been brought to light. The few remaining people of Earth already faced an enormous problem, but now they were expected to somehow magically relocate to another world. Then she took a deep breath and collected her wits before projecting, "Well if that's the case, then we are in big trouble. I don't know what to do about this, and I think that your species may have just written our epitaph here on Earth."

"Janet, as we have discussed before on many occasions, you must remain focused. Don't concede to this daunting challenge and therefore allow the stagnation of your species ongoing evolution. You must think of an alternative solution, and then do whatever is necessary to make it happen."

Janet thought for a moment, and then rose to her feet. With a regained stern resolve, she expanded her telepathic reply so that Hank and Kristyn could also hear. The projection was short, but not so sweet, "I will need a tremendous amount of help from both of you, and you may find this difficult to believe. We must leave this planet if we are to survive!"

ꝑ

CHAPTER THIRTY-ONE

A PLAN OF ACTION

The modern society of Earth had exhibited numerous examples of global cooperation throughout the most recent of centuries, and although that held true for multiple disciplines, it was especially poignant with regard to advances in engineering. As wonderful as that had been, none of those previous efforts had approached the needs of this particular endeavor. If a portion of those that remained of the human contingent on Earth were to have any hope of sustained survival, then they would need to relocate to another world. That daunting task would require undertaking not only the design and construction of a vessel that would be capable of transporting them to a different marble in space, but in also determining how to properly supply it for the voyage and needs of the subsequent new colony.

Thanks in part to the historical discs revealing Earth's previous ventures into space, and to a larger degree the more advanced unmanned probes of the modern era, a decision had been made that the logical choice for a colony would be on Mars. Although massive amounts of information had been learned about Venus during both space ages, that planet had been ruled out for a hugely significant reason. With a closer proximity to the host star than Earth, extremely high surface temperatures existed. Even with modern scientific advances, the orbital path of Venus made it unrealistic for long or even short term human habitation. As the nearest of the outward planets, that was also believed to have sustained life at one time in the distant past, Mars then became the most viable option for the historic effort.

The engineering brain trust of the planet, which now included Hank, communicated with each other on countless occasions to discuss various design specifications of what had been tabbed "The lifeboat". Their task was to design a vessel not only large enough to transport the precious cargo of human passengers, but then upon arrival subsequently become one aspect of the future habitat. Additionally, the vessel would need to contain everything necessary to ensure that the cargo at least stood a fighting chance to survive.

Hank began their most recent group conversation with, "So who knows how we are going to launch, and then obtain orbit, in such a massive vehicle?"

After a long moment of total silence followed by a few murmurs, one young engineer from Kutaisi upon the eastern shore of the enlarged former Black Sea replied, "We don't! We will need to build the lifeboat in orbit."

As the murmurs resumed, Hank glanced over at Kristyn with a smile and shrugged his shoulders. Then he looked back at the communication screen and said, "You sound quite sure of that, and it's an interesting idea. Do you have any thoughts on how we would accomplish such an undertaking?"

"Yes I do Hank. Each community would first need to construct a modified version of our existing shuttles that are capable of obtaining low Earth orbit. Then we could use those vehicles to transport the necessary materials for the assembly of our much larger lifeboat."

"That's a fantastic concept, and I really like the way you think. Thank you very much for speaking up. Now, let's begin with that aspect of the overall plan. We can tackle questions and problems associated with the lifeboat after we have figured out how to modify our existing shuttles. Can anyone else add constructive suggestions to what has been proposed?"

A young woman from Rio Paulo was first to respond. She said, "We could employ the same propulsion method for escape velocity that our exploratory probes currently use. All it would take is a modification for the larger size and payload of the shuttle."

"I agree that would be a good place to start. Will you take the lead on looking into that aspect of the modifications?"

"Certainly, I'll get started right away."

"Thank you. Now does anyone have any thoughts on how to protect the interior of the shuttles, and those who will ride in them, from the vacuum of space?"

While they were occupied with that discussion and challenge, other groups grappled with conceptual thoughts or problems with regard to the mother ship and how to make the dream of transitioning to Mars a reality. Beyond the essential questions of fuel and propulsion, the manufacturing process needed for the creation of reusable air from expended carbon dioxide needed to be addressed. Next were the medical needs, along with food, water, and even the proper use or disposal of waste products. Each team worked tirelessly on determining how much room would be needed for what they deemed to be vital for the endeavor, but the common denominator for all of them was that space would be at a premium.

Once it was agreed upon that, unlike with Colt and Hanks introduction of the SSP, there would be no cause for or the acceptance of developing any hybrid variations, work on enhancements to the shuttles could begin. A plan was devised for the various stages of the lifeboat construction, and at the suggestion of Hank, that would include the use of solar sails for a power source and eventual added propulsion. Before that could begin however, there were several other steps that needed to be taken into consideration.

First a set of four prototype shuttles, each named for their respective population centers, would be simultaneously modified in the communities of Dripping Springs, Katoomba, Maple Ridge, and Kirkwood near to where Port Elizabeth had once existed on the southern tip of the African continent. Initially, each shuttle would be designed to seat only the pilot and three others serving as added construction crew. Although that would be modified for their final voyages of transporting human cargo to the lifeboat, fabricated materials for assembly would fill much of the interior space. Each shuttle would then be required to make several roundtrips in order to assemble the framework of the main body, the sixteen docking clamps, and all but a small portion of the external and internal shells.

When that process was completed, four additional shuttles, once again named for their place of origin, would transport and install the internal operational components. Those would include the non-organic aspects pertaining to the greenhouse, hydroponics, and oxygen processing systems. The next wave of four would begin work on constructing the solar sails, as it was believed that any issues in their development would have been solved by then. Finally, the last four would complete the interior finish work which included the tightly fit sleeping, eating, and exercise areas. All told, the completion of the process was expected to take at least two years.

Knowing that they had a year or so before their aspect of the project would be needed, Hank and the few remaining engineers from what his father had referred to as "The Modern NASA" began work on the array of solar sails for the lifeboat. Initial specifications required that the sails, three on each side of the vehicle, would be much larger in square footage than the single sail used for the reconnaissance probes of Mars.

When Hank met with members of the team via the communication screen, he said, "We have been tasked with a difficult challenge, and although we supposedly have a year to prepare, I have confidence that we can accomplish our goal quicker than most would believe. If so, then perhaps we could assist with other aspects of the overall plan. With that in mind, I propose that we behave as if we have far less time than what has been allotted to us."

One of his counterparts responded with, "That sounds like good thinking to me Hank, so let's get on with it."

"Thank you. Now unless any of you have an objection, then I have an idea as to how we could position each of the sails in the array."

The momentary silence that ensued was broken only when a young woman said, "It would appear that none of us have an objection, so go ahead."

"Well alright then. How about if we were to position the three sails designated for each side of the vehicle at various protruding angles. They could all be connected along similar points of the mainframe between the docking clamps?"

A young man immediately replied, "But if we did that, wouldn't it cause some of them to block out the solar energy that we're attempting to harness?"

"Not necessarily. Imagine the most forward of the sails being positioned between the first and second docking clamps of the upper level, with the middle sail between the second and third set but in between the levels. Then the rear sail would be positioned between the third and fourth on the lower level."

"Alright, but they could still block the energy flow."

"Yes they could, if they were all deployed at the same angle. Now imagine the hours of a clock."

"What's a clock?"

"Sorry, my mom and dad told me about them. A clock is an old devise from before the apocalypse that people used so they could measure what time of the day it was."

"Why would they need to know that?"

"Well, pardon the pun, but that's probably a discussion that we should have at another time. Let me show you what I mean visually."

With that Hank stood before the viewing screen and positioned his arms in a way to demonstrate. The forward set of solar sails would be positioned from the theoretical hours of twelve over to two, then two to four for the middle, and four to six for the rear on the starboard side of the vehicle. The other three sails would be deployed in a mirror image pattern on the port side, and in so doing would create a full circle to capture the solar wind from behind.

At the completion of his explanation, the man replied, "That sounds pretty cool."

"Thank you."

Another voice entered the discussion with, "I like it too Hank, but I do think that such an arrangement could lead to a problem. What happens to the two lower sails at the rear, and the two in the middle, when the lifeboat arrives and lands on the surface of Mars?"

"Well that's a good question. Each of the sails would have already been retracted for maneuverability long before landing, but we would still face the challenge of dealing with the solid protruding arms employed as booms and masts that would extend below the horizontal axis of the lifeboat. I'm in total agreement with you that the ship couldn't possibly attempt a landing with such a configuration, so we would need to figure out some way to retract those booms and masts shortly after furling in the six solar sails. With that in mind, let's consider the floor to be open to anyone who might have a suggestion as to how we could accomplish that."

After much debate, one of the subsequently proposed solutions was agreed upon and the group communication came to a close for the day. Hank walked toward his dwelling so that he could review some design sketches, and upon his approach, heard his mother, Kristyn, and her three young siblings playing a game near the door. When he projected a greeting toward the two women, followed by a verbal acknowledgement of the three little ones, Janet quickly returned a simple projection. "The new administrator came by to see you a short time ago. He asked if you could please visit his dwelling to discuss an issue of great importance as soon as possible."

CHAPTER THIRTY-TWO
THE CHOSEN ONE

Entering the new administrator's dwelling, Hank found two men seated at the table. He recognized that one was an old friend, and it was an unexpected pleasure for Hank to see that the man had lived longer than most with the virus. Before shaking the hand of his host with a firmer grip, Hank reached for the frail hand of his former instructor. Then he accepted an offer to join them for some refreshments.

A moment later Hank heard the explanation of why he had been summoned, and all that was being asked of him. The discussion included his friend stating, "As the last of us globally who hasn't become infected, you know that you are the most logical choice for this assignment."

"Although I understand your reasoning, your extensive experience would make you the best candidate."

"That may be true, but as you can plainly see, it's just not practical for me to attempt it. My body is telling me that my time is short, and I have had a mild hallucination or two. I don't believe that I have the inner strength to complete the necessary training of the candidates before my death. Besides that Hank, you are still the best student that I ever had and you can be a very good instructor as well."

After a moment of contemplation, Hank replied, "Well alright then. Thanks for the kind words and your confidence in me. If you truly feel that strongly about it, then I'll do it."

"That's good to hear Hank. Your efforts will benefit all that remain when the time comes."

"I hope so. In order for me to properly do what you ask, then I won't be able to continue working on the solar sails for the lifeboat."

"We know that Hank, but wouldn't you agree that the solar sails would become a meaningless endeavor without any shuttle pilots to transport the materials and personnel to the lifeboat? Now, can you think of any potential candidates?"

"I understand your point, and yes, three men do come to mind instantly. Before their long term abduction by the alien species that pre-dated the apocalypse, they were pilots of ancient Earth aircraft that were vastly different than those of today. Tests have shown that the virus is completely stagnant within each of their systems, and they all have certification in our current shuttles as a result of logging extended hours. I believe that they possess the instinctive feel for what would be required to pilot a redesigned shuttle into orbit."

"That sounds like an excellent place to start, and I think that they, and you, should begin training right away. We would then have four capable pilots for the initial construction phase of the lifeboat. Now, do you have any suggestions for other people who could become pilots soon after that?"

"Based on your personal assessment of how the virus has affected you and other shuttle pilots, we must turn to those who aren't infected."

"You mean young teenagers or children? Impossible."

"No. Although that may become a reality eventually, for now I was thinking that we should consider the Mayans. There are twenty-one of them, and they are all healthy adults. I believe that several would make excellent candidates, and just like me and the three pilots, they have been in space!"

"Alright, if you think they would be willing. We could start by identifying which of the population centers the Mayans were sent to, and get them back here as soon as possible?"

"Each population center has at least one of the Mayans living there. I remember that Ross and Aurora wanted to make sure of that when everyone was distributed, and Kristyn can verify that with Aurora's original records. But I was thinking that instead of wasting precious time by bringing them here, perhaps we could begin their instructional process at their respective population centers. They could at least learn the basics of the current shuttles from any pilots who are still alive, and then we could send for them later. After all, we don't really need them to be totally proficient right away do we? If not, then why move them twice if we don't have to?"

"That's a good point."

"Well alright then. Why don't I just start with my own training, and that of the three former pilots that I spoke of? Each of us has much to learn and little time to work with."

"Fair enough, let's get them here."

"Good. Now I do have one other point to make. It has been determined that a four person crew in each shuttle will handle the early construction of the lifeboat."

"That's true."

"Well I propose that the four of us who will receive the initial training should also become the crew of that first mission. Each of us will need to get a feel for the shuttle, and collectively work out any issues that may not have been addressed in the simulator phase of training. I believe that process should take place before each of us has also become responsible for three additional passengers."

"That sounds like a good idea Hank, but you wouldn't be able to begin construction. The plan calls for all four of the shuttles to rendezvous in orbit when construction begins. Your point is well taken though, so we will schedule an orbital flight for the four of you when training is complete."

"Alright that sounds fair. But when the four shuttles rendezvous, I think that the construction crews of each should be some of the

Mayans. By then they will be partially versed in flight operations, and they will need some time in space to acquire a feel for the shuttles just as we will."

"I agree Hank, that's a good plan of action. Now you said that Kristyn could locate the three pilots and certain others for us."

"Yes she can, although I already know where one of the men I speak of is located. I remember seeing him a few years ago on the communication screen when my father and I were discussing improvements to the SSP. As for the others, Kristyn is the one we should consult with."

With that Hank somewhat reluctantly accepted the task as the chosen one, and he felt bad that in so doing his former mentor had also accepted his limitations and ultimate fate. The man had been a good friend since the earliest weeks of Hank's life on Earth, and had graciously answered all of the operational questions presented to him while returning from the Cheyenne Mountain museum complex. Sometime later, when Colt had realized that his son might possess an aptitude for such things, the man gladly stepped in as the primary instructor during Hank's quest for certification as a shuttle pilot.

At the conclusion of their discussion, Hank bid his friend farewell for what he knew in his heart to be the last time. Then he walked outside with the administrator, who thanks largely to Janet's initial influence, had become more comfortable with his various responsibilities.

When they reached a safe distance, Hank said, "He doesn't have much time left I'm afraid."

"That's why we summoned you so urgently. He's quite aware that action is needed immediately, and that he has no hope of surviving long enough to see the training through."

"I understand."

"He has unwavering belief in your ability to complete this task, and specifically requested that you be the first one it was offered to. Hank, you need to know that I concur with his assessment. I know you can do this."

"Thanks, I'll try not to let you down."

Although he promised the administrator that he would contact Kristyn about the need for locating the pilots, Hank had never said how he would do so. He knew within himself that it wasn't really necessary to physically go inform her, and his initial impulse was to simply project a message toward her. But in truth, Hank also knew that a visit with Kristyn was never a bad thing. With that thought now controlling his actions, he decided that he could also maintain their joint cover by walking toward the communication center.

Along the way, he projected a message toward the three pilots. "Hello gentlemen, this is Hank. I have something important to discuss with each of you. There has been a new development with the plans of the lifeboat, and it will directly involve the four of us. I have been pulled away from the solar sail project, and have accepted the task of learning how to fly the redesigned shuttle into orbit. Additionally, I recommended that the three of you join me in the training. A decision has been reached that we shall become the first wave of those shuttle pilots, and we will then instruct others to follow. I felt it was important to provide you with advance knowledge, but in order to maintain the established cover, Kristyn will be in contact with your various population centers. On behalf of the administrative team, she will be submitting instructions that each of you will be required to report to Dripping Springs as soon as possible."

CHAPTER THIRTY-THREE

TRAINING WHEELS

Joseph finally arrived via the long shuttle flight from Katoomba, and then joined the other two pilots from the time of old Earth to begin training for their upcoming multiple space flights. Each of the men had piloted the older transit shuttles toward the training rendezvous in order to shake off some personal rust and gain additional hours of flight time, but that action would have little or no impact on what lay ahead. After welcoming the latest arrival, Hank offered him food and drink.

The reunion for the three pilots was an inspiring sight to witness, as it had been ten years since all of them had been together. They provided Hank with an instant reminder of the brotherhood that they shared, and he flashed back to how each of the fourteen pilots and crew members of Flight 19 had interacted with one another back on ₹-593-ℨπ-2-2.

That group of men, each with their own individual story, had endured so much throughout the days of old Earth's largest and most horrifically bloody conflict. Then came their years of long term captivity after the alien abduction, joining Ross on his pilgrimage to establish a new human colony with the help of those same aliens in some faraway solar system, and then finally, at least for these three, volunteering as recruits to venture back to Earth for yet another cause. Now Hank would pool his talents with theirs in the latest endeavor to relocate a few lucky souls to Mars, and he was respectfully in awe to be in such company. Those three men were the real heroes, and Hank knew it.

When the reunion was concluded and each of the three men had playfully commented on how the past ten years had negatively impacted the other two, they all noticed that the most dramatic difference had occurred within Hank. Although upon occasion he had briefly appeared on the screen via the communication system, none of them had really seen Hank since he was only eight years old. Now eighteen, there had obviously been changes. Hank had reached the height of his father Colt, and had filled out some with muscular tone.

One of them said, "I must admit Hank, when you telepathically informed me that you would be the primary instructor for these missions, I was concerned. Although I was aware from our shared telepathy that you were bright, I also kept visualizing you as the boy I knew ten years ago. Now it's obvious that you're not that little anymore, so I gladly stand corrected."

Hank decided that it would be a good opportunity to establish a playful banter as the three of them had done, and hoped they would accept him deeper into the fold for it. He replied, "Don't worry, there's nothing to forgive. I had pictured you as still being the young pilot that I once knew."

His intent had been properly received, as each of the other two men began to laugh. Then the one who the remark had been aimed at smiled and said, "Alright, you owed me that one. Good job Hank."

"Thanks."

With that behind them, the four of them were eager to get to work. Before they could begin though, they all received telepathy from Janet. She projected, "It's wonderful that all of you could get together and work on this vital aspect of our intended plan. There are no others that I would prefer to have in your place. Please keep each other safe for the benefit of those who care about you, and for those who will count upon you. I know within my heart that you will succeed."

Joseph was first to verbally respond by saying, "That was a good pep talk to get us all motivated."

Hank replied, "I think so too, and let's all do our best to substantiate everyone's belief in us by getting to work?"

Throughout the following month, it became obvious that their collective advance knowledge of flight operations helped with the training. As they spent countless hours in the simulator, each man learned of and practiced all of the duties and responsibilities that came with both of the front seats. While rotating through those seats, or observing from the two crew seats behind, the group continuously bounced ideas off one another to improve their collective performance. That process also included the development of instructional discs that would be employed as one of the many training tools for the following wave of candidates.

It was suggested, and somewhat reluctantly agreed upon, that an entire training day within the simulator should focus on identifying what would make the shuttle crash. There was a method to the madness however, as that information would be vital for the upcoming pilots. After all, if one of them crashed during the construction phase, then both the shuttle along with the pilot and crew would need to be replaced. If such a case were to occur, the parts to replace the shuttle could be refabricated. Unfortunately, there just weren't that many viable candidates to replace the loss of four souls who were either pilots or able bodied members of a construction crew. Beyond that obvious predicament, if the mishap were to occur during final ascension to the lifeboat, then there would be no such luxury. The precious cargo needed for the group effort would be irreplaceably lost.

At the completion of their first month of training, a short rest break had been earned. Hank seized the opportunity to provide his three friends with a ride on his SSP, and Kristyn came along with them. After a few hours of fun, Hank said, "Hey, would anybody like to see what progress has been made with the modifications to the new shuttle?"

A resounding positive response was all he needed to hear, so Hank turned toward the construction facility. As they looked over both the external and internal areas of the craft, Kristyn could hear the collective thoughts of the four men. Their desire to fly the shuttle into space was overpowering, so she needed to project to them, "Would all of you just calm down a little bit. You will all get your chance to fly one of these soon enough."

Her timely premonition was then proven to be correct, as the engineer in charge of construction informed them that the first of the redesigned shuttles would be available for launch and orbital testing within another week.

Hank did not hesitate to respond to the man's claim, as he said, "None of the four of us will require any additional time to train beyond that day, and we will all be ready when you are for the inaugural flight."

ʆ

CHAPTER THIRTY-FOUR

EXTENDED RANKS

Hank felt the comfort of the pilot's seat beneath him, and gazed upon the bright and clean instrument panel of the newly redesigned shuttle. Then after rubbing the emblem of his necklace for good luck as Ross had always done just before a flight, Hank tucked it back into his shirt. Then turning toward each of his three crew mates, he asked, "Is everyone ready?"

After receiving a positive nod from each of them, Hank pushed the throttles slightly forward. As the shuttle lifted a few feet from its horizontal resting position without a sound, and then moved beyond the beach toward the plentiful refueling source of the ocean's salt water, Janet crossed her fingers. She then projected at Kristyn, "I hope that the name of our new shuttle doesn't become a representation of its performance."

Kristyn couldn't help but smile at Janet's thought, and wondered if anyone else felt the same, as the huge lettering on the side of it read, "Dripping Springs". Then she projected only to Hank, "Have fun, but please be careful."

Hank responded with, "Thanks Kristyn, I will. See you in a couple of days."

The shuttle then lowered to rest upon the placid ocean surface just beyond the line of small surf. A moment later it rose to hover briefly, and then sped away from the coast while in horizontal flight. As Hank pushed the throttles forward for additional speed, Joseph looked at the instruments before him and confirmed, "The venting design appears to be functioning properly. We are getting a positive reading that the turbines between the external and internal shells of the fuselage are collecting the wind and transferring it into storable power."

Mimicking a phrase that each of the pilots had uttered in his presence on multiple occasions, Hank responded with, "Roger that Joseph. That's good news."

Joseph asked, "What's our speed now?"

"We're almost there, just a few more seconds."

The two pilots located in the seats directly behind Hank and Joseph braced for the upcoming maneuver and waited. They soon felt the force of being pushed deeper into their seats, as Hank pulled back on the handles and the shuttle moved skyward. Climbing at an ever increasing angle, Hank pushed forward on the throttles to unleash additional thrust. The shuttle responded in kind, and before it shot through the outer atmosphere Hank exclaimed, "Here we go!"

Seconds later they all began to feel a decrease in their weight as they entered space, and Joseph said, "Wow! That was fun."

A pilot from the rear seats added, "It sure was."

Hank replied, "I agree, and I think that each of you will enjoy the ride even more when you try it from this seat!"

The forth man then said, "I'm sure you're right, and I can't wait to fly one of these into orbit!"

The next few minutes were spent doing little more than enjoying the view, as they began their initial orbit of the Earth below. Hank didn't know it, and he never would, but he had just joined Ross in one of those "first ever" moments in the human space endeavor. Unlike during the era of the former space program, Hank had just launched a manned spacecraft into orbit from a horizontal starting position on

Earth. When Ross had performed the first horizontal liftoff with a shuttle built during the late twentieth century, he had done so from the surface of Earth's now extinct moon.

At the completion of their first orbit, Hank said, "Well each of has some maneuvers to practice, and our solar panels will enable us to stay up here until we get it right. Who wants to go first?"

Two days later, Janet watched as the shuttle returned to Dripping Springs with a smooth horizontal approach. They were able to re-enter the atmosphere at nearly a sixty degree angle, which was roughly the same as the departure trajectory used to escape it. There had been minimal discomfort of heat or turbulence during the return, and the collective opinion of the four pilots was that nearly any angle of re-entry could be attempted. Hank, perhaps not alone in his belief, felt that re-entry was the most fun aspect of the flight, as he had the shuttle sharply nosed down. Once they were safely through the atmosphere, pulling back on the handles to begin the leveling out process was required. It took some time, but eventually the shuttle was flying in a horizontal position and remained that way for nearly an hour before arriving back at Dripping Springs. Although useless within the vacuum of space, the vents forcing air into the turbines had once again harnessed power during the descent and approach to the launch site.

The crew began to discuss and compare the data that had been collectively obtained during their journey, but before they were prepared to disembark, they heard a projection. Janet's thoughts were loud and clear, "Did everything go alright? You had us all worried because you were up there a little longer than expected."

Joseph turned to Hank and verbally asked, "Do you want to handle this one?"

"Sure, I'll take care of it."

Then Hank projected so that the three members of his crew and Janet could hear, "Please don't do that mom. You had the ability to track our position via the orbiting satellites, and you could have telepathically communicated with us as a group or individually whenever you wanted to. But if you must know, then yes mother, everything went fine. We all played well with others, had a good time, and we're sorry to be late. You also don't have to worry, because I ate all of my vegetables."

The deafening silence that followed his telepathy was broken only by the laughter within the shuttle. Hank knew that he had probably made his mother angry, but it was worth it. The past few days had solidified his place within a group that he had aspired to be a part of for many years. He was now a full-fledged shuttle pilot within the eyes of men who had been pilots during a much more heroic era, and he was proud of that personal achievement.

CHAPTER THIRTY-FIVE

CONSTRUCTION ZONE

While positioned in space directly above the northern pole as the first three segments of their intended diamond formation, the Katoomba, Kirkwood, and Maple Ridge awaited the arrival of the fourth shuttle. A moment later Joseph could see the approaching Dripping Springs rising from below, and projected to the pilots and their Mayan crews who were in training to become the next wave of such, "There she is now, and as usual, Hank is right on schedule."

After pulling into position to complete the diamond, Hank projected, "Well alright then. Thanks for waiting, should we get started?"

Then he eased the Dripping Springs forward and the others followed suit. When the spacing between the noses of each shuttle became optimal, the forward momentum was halted. A short time later the men and women aboard the spacecraft emerged from various hatches with pre-fabricated sections of the mainframe, and began the painstaking process of assembling them. The work continued for the better part of two days until no cargo remained within the holds of all four shuttles, but the double deck nose section had begun to take shape. With the process scheduled to repeat itself throughout several upcoming missions, it would take months before the entirety of the basic mainframe could be completed. Only then would they move on to phase two with additional help.

During the third such rendezvous in orbit, sections just aft of what would eventually serve as the flight deck area were fitted into place. On both the port and starboard side of the now recognizable double deck nose section of the lifeboat, the first two of sixteen sets of docking clamps were ready to be tested. With no others aboard, Hank moved the Dripping Springs into a position that was parallel with the awaiting clamps. Then with a gentle touch of the thrusters, the shuttle slid over until Hank felt the slightest bump. The clamps locked him in place, and he projected, "How's it look Joseph?"

"It looks good Hank. Give me a minute to get a reading on the overall structure. I want to make sure that the gentle nudge from the shuttle won't reposition the entire mass."

"Roger that."

Within minutes Joseph, who like Hank had temporarily transferred his crew to one of the other two shuttles, had reported that all remained unchanged. He would then proceed with the Katoomba toward the opposite docking clamp. Once secure, he projected, "This is good progress to have these two sets of clamps in place and operational after just three missions. The lifeboat is beginning to take shape."

Hank replied, "Yes she is, but we still have a long way to go. Now just imagine the overall size being about five times larger than what we have already assembled."

With the Kirkwood and Maple Ridge in position just meters off the aft end of the docking clamps, all fourteen men and women within them began to spill out to continue what had been started. The efforts needed to add length to the mainframe behind the first of the docking clamps would be addressed during the fourth mission in a few days', but what remained of this cargo was destined for the nose section. Resembling bees working on the hive, work began on closing in the area around the nose section and flight deck. Pre-fabricated panels intended for both the external and internal shells, along with the dense insulation layer that would be sandwiched between, were fit in like pieces of an old fashioned puzzle. Shared alien technology then came into play, as a substance with a consistency similar to cold honey was applied to all the seams both inside and out.

Via the first of many telepathic conversations that transpired soon after learning that ₹-593-ᢒπ-2-2 would not become part of the equation; Hank had been informed by their alien friend to be liberal with the application. The semi-liquid substance that he and others were applying to the lifeboat had been developed by the alien species during the early days of their exploration of space, and they gladly shared that ancient technology of how to manufacture it from elements found on Earth as well as many other worlds. Behaving like a form of liquid metal, the substance penetrated any seams that might be present within the framework of a spacecraft. Then it would harden into an invisible layer. Supposedly it didn't matter if the application took place within atmospheric conditions or in the vacuum of space; the results would be the same. Some had been skeptical at first, but tests on Earth led to a continuous solid piece of shell. The current work had become the first application in space for humans, and Hank, Joseph, and the others could now confirm that whatever the stuff was, it worked really well. Although unwilling to provide the humans with transport to another world, the alien species had shared a substance that could help with the intended endeavor.

Before moving back into the Dripping Springs with the three Mayan members of his crew, Hank marveled at the progress that had been made on this mission alone. Not only could two shuttles now dock whenever on site, but the three layers of non-distortion glass that created a large curved viewing portal from the flight deck were now securely in place. Hank projected toward those present within each of the four shuttles, "This is going well so far, and I thank you all for your hard work and effort. Now let's all head back to rest and get another load of cargo. The sooner we get back up here, the sooner we can complete the mainframe of the lifeboat."

ᢒ

CHAPTER THIRTY-SIX

INTERNAL MECHANICS

Standing in the manufacturing facility with a handful of his co-inventors, one engineer said, "I think that we have finally figured it out!"

Another replied, "I agree with you. This new design of ours will create nearly the same output as the older version, while also being compact enough to fit well within the limited space that we have been allocated."

With that the troublesome question of the hydroponic system needed for use in the essential greenhouse had been successfully addressed, and it would fit harmoniously next to the water purification system when the time arrived. That question of purification had initially been thought to be a more daunting challenge than the distribution, as a major shift in what needed to be purified became the ultimate concern. Once the original supply of ocean saltwater within both the holding tanks of the lifeboat and those of the shuttles had been purified and consumed through various ways, then only a supplemental purification process could provide an additional supply. Both the gray water and wastewater would need to go through an extensive process before it could be considered potable and therefore suitable for human consumption. As a consequence, a process needed to be developed that could purify water from a natural state as well as one that had run through the human body.

The concept of such a process was something that the society of new Earth had never remotely considered, because they had always just desalinated the seemingly endless supply of ocean saltwater for their consumption needs. Sadly, that lack of vision was quite similar to the values of the late twentieth or early twenty-first century in the decades leading up to the apocalypse. At that time in human history, in spite of strong evidence to prove otherwise, a significant majority of the ever-expanding population considered the natural resources of the planet to be something limitless in scope.

Fortunately in the present day, the engineers assigned to the project of water purification had come through quickly, and had disproved the general consensus that their task would be more difficult than that of distributing the essential product. Conversely, those assigned to the relatively easy project of hydroponics had dragged their feet somewhat. Now a year into construction of the lifeboat, each of those vital systems could be installed at any time.

Janet walked into the communication center and found one of Kristyn's young protégés at the main consul. She said, "Good morning. Could you please help me contact Crewe, or should I locate Kristyn to do it?"

From another section of the facility, Kristyn replied, "Hello Janet. He is quite qualified to contact them for you. Just tell him who in Crewe that you need to speak with, and then sit back and relax for a minute."

Turning back to the young boy, Janet said, "Can you get me the administrator of the community first, and then I would like to also speak with the lead engineer of the manufacturing facility."

Barely twenty and known to be deep into the infection stage, the latest in a line of very youthful administrators within Crewe soon appeared on the screen. Although pleasant enough in his approach to the job, the man was serving more in a compulsory role for the community as opposed to one of benefit. He truly had no clue as to what was required of him. In typical fashion, he said, "Good day to you Janet. Are things well in Dripping Springs?"

She thought, are things well? It was a rather ridiculous question in light of the global epidemic, and the time sensitive nature with regard to the pending departure from Earth, but it went in line with his oblivious nature. "We're fine today thanks. How are you?"

"Oh getting on as they say. What can I do for you?"

"I'm checking on the progress of your engineering team. You know that they are working on the last element of phase two for the lifeboat, and it needs to be completed before we can move forward."

"Yes indeed. Well let me go check on that for you, and we will get back in touch soon."

With that the screen went blank, and Janet felt yet another level of frustration. The young boy seated next to her said, "I can contact Crewe again if you want me to. Then at least when he comes back we will already be connected."

"That would be great, and thanks."

When the administrator entered the room, the smiles on the faces of the engineering collective should have been evidence sufficient to answer Janet's inquiry, but he somehow missed it. Then he said, "Janet in Dripping Springs has been in contact with me again, so how's it coming along?"

The oldest of the group, knowing well of the young administrators short coming replied, "I will talk to her for you if you would like. We have some good news for her. This model that we have just completed will work better than any of the previous versions."

A short time later Janet received the report from the young lady via the communication screen, and she responded with, "That's good to hear, and I have faith in your collective abilities. I'm sure that it will suit our needs."

"Thank you."

"Now, how soon can you get the machinery loaded onto your shuttle? Hank has informed me that assembly of the added propulsion system is waiting for the final segment of the hull to be sealed. That can't begin until all of the internal machinery and hardware has been placed within. In short, we can't move forward until the Crewe delivers your payload!"

"I understand Janet, and I'm sorry if we have slowed things down a bit. I will have some of my colleagues load the hydroponics system onto the shuttle straight away, and then I'll ask the pilot to launch as soon as he is ready."

With that the new hydroponics system was moved onto a nearby version of the SST, and transported to the awaiting shuttle. The pilot of the Crewe, trained by Hank, was waiting eagerly for them. He played it off as if he was unaware, but Janet had already telepathically informed him that the payload was coming his way. He watched as they loaded the machinery aboard, and then he began his pre-flight checklist.

Several hours later, while visualizing a fully deployed solar sail array from his hovering position aft of the lifeboat, Hank received a projection from his former Mayan student. The man had been a major asset during the assembly of the hull and docking clamps, and was now proving that he had been the correct choice as a candidate to pilot the shuttle for his population center. Now on his third flight up with cargo from the former British Isles, he was reporting that the Crewe had just passed through the upper atmosphere and would arrive at the lifeboat shortly.

After maneuvering toward one of the vacant docking clamps, Hank then suited up for another walk within the still non-atmospheric confines of the hull. When the cargo from the Crewe was brought through the only opening that remained in the mainframe, Hanks reaction was one of bewilderment. He then asked, "What is this thing?"

His student responded verbally, "I have been informed that this is the new and improved version of the hydroponics system."

Hank was amazed, and although he didn't doubt that the information he had just been given was what had been conveyed to the Mayan pilot, he quickly projected to Janet, "Hey mom. Are the engineers from Crewe on the level with what they have just delivered?"

"What do you mean?"

"The payload that they sent us must be incomplete."

"Well I'm told it's the new and improved hydroponics system. Why? There's not some problem with it is there? Was it damaged during transit?"

"No. It's not broken or damaged as far as I can tell, and your words do echo those of the Mayan pilot who delivered the payload."

"Well then what is it Hank?"

"It's just that the machinery is so much more compact than any other version that I have seen before."

"Well I suppose that would be a good thing given the amount of space available in the lifeboat. Besides, they claim it will be better than any model before it, and I don't really care about the size of the machine as long as it works!"

"That's true. But what if it doesn't produce enough output, or worse, doesn't work at all? In that event maintaining our food supply would become an even bigger challenge than we had originally thought."

ꝭ

CHAPTER THIRTY-SEVEN

MYSTERY DESCENDANT

A few months later, with several more missions behind him, Hank moved back inside the Dripping Springs. He was quite pleased with the work that had just been completed, as the last pair of the six solar sails and their accompanying boom and mast structures were now fully connected to the lifeboat. The men and women who had performed the task had done an excellent job, and had earned the right to revel in their success. Installing this most recent pair had definitely been the easiest of the six, and Hank was glad to have it that way. As the most forward set, they would be positioned on the hours of the clock from ten through twelve, and twelve through two once they were deployed. That also meant that their respective booms and masts wouldn't require retraction before landing on Mars.

While waiting for his three construction crewmates to return to the shuttle and relax, Hank decided to practice with his long range telepathic ability. On previous missions he had always communicated with those working on constructing the lifeboat, or others such as Janet or Kristyn on the planet surface below. Although he had projected with the alien on several occasions while resting between missions in Dripping Springs, Hank now finally had the opportunity to communicate with his friend while in orbit. With a determined focus that his mother Janet had instilled upon him throughout her many lessons of telepathy, Hank projected, "Can you hear me out there?"

Nothing came back, so he tried again, "Hello my alien friend, this is Hank. Can you hear me?"

The response was then quick, and showed a measure of good humor that may have been learned while sharing a friendship with Ross. The alien projected, "It has always been my practice to never respond to a human unless they identify who they are first, but yes Hank, I can hear you. Oh and by the way, stop screaming at me."

After a slight laugh, Hank replied "Sorry about that."

"It's alright Hank, besides it shows me that you have been practicing. Your projection strength is much better than when we last communicated.

"Thanks."

"Is there something that I can help you with?"

"Perhaps, I mean, I don't really know."

Having observed Hank upon occasion throughout his short human lifespan, it was known that he was rarely, if ever, at a loss for words or direction of his thoughts. That trait had continued as Hank developed his ability to project, so the alien sensed that something was distracting the young man. He then projected, "You seem troubled Hank. What's on your mind?"

"Well, as we move closer and closer to our planned departure from Earth, I have been thinking about all that has transpired since you brought us here."

"That would seem to be normal for your species."

"Yes it is, but those memories reminded me of a place that a few of us visited with Ross and a possibility that I raised at that time. Although I forgot about it for several years, the thought of it has resurfaced lately. I was wondering if perhaps you could help me to know the truth."

"I understand, so what was this possibility that you are referring to?"

"When my father discovered the exhibit for Ross in the Cheyenne Mountain museum complex, and that some of the items within the display had been donated by members of Ross's family who had survived the apocalypse, I wondered if there might be someone within the population of new Earth who had descended from those survivors. In essence, did we have a distant relative living among us?"

"And you seek the answer to that question now?"

"Well, yes. Can you help me with that?"

"Are you sure that you want to know?"

"Sure, what harm could it do?"

"Alright, then yes I can help you Hank. You did indeed have a distant relative who descended from Ross and his wife Patty. As only one of their offspring had offspring of their own, that daughter was the root of the modern day citizen whom you seek."

"Well that's cool, but you said that I did have a distant relative. Is that person dead now?"

"Yes Hank. I'm sorry, but she is. She died several years ago at the hands of the virus."

"She died. That's a shame; I would have liked to have met her and, if possible, become friends."

"But you did know her Hank, and you were friends. In fact, you met her for the first time on the day that you arrived."

"I did? You mean that she was right here in Dripping Springs all the time and Ross never knew it? Who was she?"

"Her name was Tori Nobles."

ᛘ

CHAPTER THIRTY-EIGHT
GENETICALLY FOCUSED

Janet initiated telepathic contact with her alien friend again, as she needed additional guidance. She, although not entirely alone in the endeavor, was laboring over the most difficult decision that any supposed leader could face. How Janet would address the all-encompassing question of another person's life versus their death could not be taken lightly, but for the vast majority of the population, that question had already been answered. The inevitable outcome of death that awaited every member of the human species had, at least on Earth, been accelerated as a consequence of the virus. She could still hope to do something for the children of the world though, but Janet felt uneasy about what fate awaited some of those who were not yet infected.

Although the lifeboat construction was now only a few months away from completion, there remained the taxing question of who would be on the passenger manifest. There simply wasn't enough room for every one of the children who were still free of the virus, so unfortunately, some of them would need to be left behind. Those unlucky souls would then contract the virus and eventually perish. Janet pondered that quandary, and the unusual twist in the odyssey that Hank had learned from the alien, as she had recently replaced yet another youthful administrator that had fallen prey to the virus. In so doing, she had assumed the position that had once belonged to Tori, who was her own descendant of more than twenty-six centuries and countless generations.

In seeking the advice from her alien friend, Janet then projected quite plainly, "This is the most horrific of decisions that I have ever been made to be part of. How can I possibly decide which of the children of my species should not be given at least a fighting chance of survival?"

Having listened to Janet's quandary, her longtime alien friend then experienced a feeling of sympathy toward her. The magnitude of her question was perhaps unequaled for any species, and the solution of such was rarely an easy one. He projected, "I understand that this current challenge is most difficult for you and other members of your species to fully comprehend, but focus remains the primary necessity when searching for the answers to your plight."

At that point Janet lost her cool, and she was hopeful that her projection toward the alien would be heard with the same volume and frustration with which it was intended. In Janet's mind she screamed, "I'm getting really tired of being told that I need to focus! I have been doing everything that I can to rectify this never ending problem from the beginning, and every time that I come to a stumbling block, all you can project at me is, stay focused! I'm starting to realize that Ross had it easy. Both times that he was faced with relocating a segment of the population; all that he needed to do was figure out who wanted to go along with him. He was never faced with the question of who he had to leave behind to die. So I say enough of the need for me to focus already, what I really need is some help!"

Realizing that she was nearing the breaking point, the alien knew that he needed to tread lightly. If Janet went over the edge, then the entirety of the plan to save this portion of humanity could fall apart. He projected, "I realize that you are facing the most difficult of decisions regarding the youth of your species, and it's true, on the relocation from ₹-593-Зúπ-2-2 back to this world Ross was only searching for those who wished to make the journey. If it will help you Janet, then rest assured that the thriving population of humans back on that moon remains both vibrant and healthy. Your species as you knew it during the time of your youth on this world, and on that moon, will continue to prosper, and at least for the foreseeable future, is safe from total extinction. As to the first of Ross's relocation efforts to that moon from this world, he faced many decisions that were just as difficult, or more so, as those that you face now. There were literally billions of your species who initially thought him to be insane when he spoke of a pending asteroid that could destroy this planet, and how he learned of it from me. It required true strength of character for Ross to look beyond that and orchestrate a plan that would ensure at least a portion of those same people could survive. One aspect of why he could sustain the extreme weight and burden of that time in your history was due to being a product of you. You need to give him credit for standing up to the daunting challenges that confronted him, and then give yourself some credit for passing on your wisdom and other gifts to him."

"But because of your species intervention, I wasn't even around for much of Ross's life. I don't understand how I could have passed on any of my so called gifts to him?"

"You can understand it Janet, if you will just allow that process to transpire. Unfortunately in order for you to move forward, you would be required to do something that you have little desire to do at this time."

"Oh, let me guess. Stay focused right?"

"Please Janet. I'm trying to help."

After a moment of self-reflection, and collection, Janet projected, "Alright, thanks for letting me know that those of my species still on that moon are thriving. It's good news, really. But my concern now rests with those of us here."

"That's what I'm trying to help you with. I would like you to stop thinking in terms of how your human society would have looked at the situation before the apocalypse or anytime in the centuries preceding that event. It won't help you to think of those on ₹-593-३ง₸-2-2 either, as they would handle things in much the same way. Although your modern colony there has been somewhat integrated with those from a previous time within the human evolution, it provides no guarantee that they have adapted to the same mindset of those earlier cultures. Some of them may have viewed this situation that you now confront in a more pragmatic way. Your species on this world has evolved in many ways since the century of your birth, and now you, and others, have begun phasing your kind into a greater leap forward. Unfortunately you are still looking at it from the perspective of everyone needing to survive in order to obtain that progression. Your personal understanding of the true meaning as to who among your species must live, as opposed to who among you might perish, is far more important with regard to the evolutionary shift and the accompanying advancement that awaits each of your survivors."

Janet had listened intently to all that had been conveyed by the alien, but had not regained her focus. Then she curtly replied, "So when all is said and done, it boils down to nothing more than the law of the jungle."

"I do not understand what you mean by that Janet. What is this law of the jungle that you speak of?"

"It's an old Earth term. It means that only the strong will survive, and the weak must perish?"

"There could be a measure of truth to that belief, but for each and every species within the universe I suppose that would depend largely on interpretation."

"Well our species doesn't work that way. The strong don't always survive, and the weak don't always perish."

"Fair enough, but you know that those of you that are still alive here on Earth will need to address that fate in some respect very soon. So at the risk of upsetting you again, I ask you to stay focused. I just provided you with another clue, so I want you to think about who within your human contingent, upon this world only, are special above the rest, and why?"

As if that question hadn't already become a significant aspect of her everyday thinking during recent months, Janet allowed it to swim around in her cranium once again. The answer to the aliens question became a growing list, and as someone who had always been rather humble, she resisted the necessity of adding her own name to that select group. Then she began with, "So the twenty-one Mayans are special."

"That's true, but why?"

"Well for several reasons I think, but it starts with their immunity and then goes to their ability to receive and project telepathically. Beyond that, the fact that they are adults would make them special in our dwindling population."

"All that is true Janet, but there is another reason that we will get to in a minute that is just as important. Now, who else do you know that will be important to your future?"

"I suppose for nearly the same reasons, the five of us who were long term abductees. We don't possess immunity, but the virus has become stagnant in all of us."

"Yes indeed. Now Janet, follow a similar line of logic to those that you have mentioned, and then identify who else would be added to your list?"

"Well, although they are both just young adults at this point, Hank and Kristyn do possess the same attributes of immunity and two way telepathy as was mentioned with the Mayan's."

"That's true. So is there anyone else?"

Janet then, as had been done many times before, pondered the thought. It was only when she accessed the content of their current conversation and the involvement of Ross that it suddenly came to her. She then projected, "Well if I were to remain focused as you so often desire, then I would have to say that Ross had something to do with it."

"Yes Janet, go on."

"I think that your clue was that Ross was a special man in part because he was a product of me. With that said, I could surmise that genetics can play a part in this equation after all."

"That would be a logical path for you to follow. Now continue."

"So based on your response to that thought, genetics must be a significant factor. Now with Ross it wouldn't be due to something happening to my genetic code while I was one of your long term abductees, as he was born before then. The same could be said for Jessica, if she possesses any telepathic projection abilities that she is unaware of. Hank is a different matter though, as he is the only of my three children that is confirmed to have two way telepathic abilities. Therefore, in keeping with the spirit of your favorite phrase, I need to focus on that. My abduction could have played a role with regard to Hank, but that would in turn make your clue of Ross being special an irrelevant point. Since my two sons do have different fathers, I could surmise that it was only my part of the genetic code that impacted their respective development."

"That's very good Janet, very good indeed. But don't stop there, keep going."

"Alright, if that's true, then it would also mean that any of the offspring from those of us who can receive and project telepathically might also be significant."

"Now you're getting there. Please continue."

"So if we are to choose some of the children or pre-teens that must stay behind, we must ensure that those who were born to a now tele-pathic parent are not among them."

"Yes, so how do you go about that?"

"I must contact Kristyn, and consult with her. We need to identify via the record keeping of Aurora, Natiya, and now Kristyn who has been born to a Mayan mother or father."

"Yes Janet, and who else?"

"Well, the same could be said for any of the children born from the efforts of the three Flight 19 pilots or Brittany."

"That's correct. Now that should make your decision a little eas-ier as to who will go on the journey. Those children or pre-teens must go with you along with those on the list of other special people that you have identified and helped to develop. As for the other young members of your species, take who you think could be beneficial for child bearing purposes in the long term, but only those that you have room for."

"We would need to develop a fair system of selection for every-one who hasn't been identified during this discussion. Otherwise there could be some sort of ugly revolt during the last days and hours before our departure."

"Don't be so sure about that Janet. Another aspect of your species evolutionary shift throughout recent centuries of your time is the lack of selfishness. If you would take a moment to think about it, you have been witness to that attribute on countless occasions since your return to Earth. What you need to do now is have a little faith in those who will not be chosen to depart with you. You must inform all that remain of your species here on Earth of your two way telepathic abilities, and of the others who, like you, possess that same evolutionary advancement. You must also disclose why certain of the youth are venturing forward, while others will be left behind. The task will not be as difficult as you believe, and you know that each and every one of your brethren deserves that level of respect. In so doing, they will be provided with one final opportunity to exhibit their enlightened trait of selflessness."

CHAPTER THIRTY-NINE

COUNCIL CHAMBERS

"You are disturbing our solitude again brother. Why do you seek an audience with the high council? Have we not just attended to your needs?"

Standing humbly before the seven members of the high council with an escort once again by his side, Janet's alien friend projected, "I have more important information to share with you about ₹-829-ᴣπ-3."

"We have just covered that topic brother, and it is not necessary for you to provide further important information. Permission has been granted to you by this council to go and investigate that system, so be on your way. You claimed that time was of the essence, so why have you not yet begun that mission?"

Staring for a moment in bewilderment, he noticed that the other six members of the council had all turned toward the leader. Then before he could respond to the question, he heard the telepathy of, "Number one, with your permission I would like to respond for our brother who stands before us."

Looking to his left, the leader replied, "I don't know why you would have such a desire number two, but if that is what you wish to do, then go ahead."

After a respectful nod, number two looked at their brother before them and projected for all to hear, "Is it correct that you have already returned from system ₹-829?"

"Yes. I have."

"And did the mission go well?"

"Yes it did, and I have much to report."

"Then do you believe that the situation on ₹-829-ᲚᴨT-3 can still be salvaged?"

"Yes I do, and with the most optimum of results."

"Interesting, explain why you believe that my brother?"

"In the seven Earth years that were required for me to make the voyage, further study and assist them for one of those years, and then return to our home world, there has been a metamorphosis within a select few of them."

"That is good news, so they can be saved."

"Yes, and one of their elders has put most of the pieces together. She understands that they must vacate the planet for continued survival, and her species is currently nearing the moment of making that a reality."

"And you know this how?"

"She has continued to telepathically communicate with me, and she has provided several reports of their progress within those projections."

Number one interjected by projecting, "Why are you attempting to deceive us brother. That is most foolish of you, and it will not be tolerated. It was only a short time ago that you stood before this esteemed council and begged us to consider your plan of action."

Having no desire to create an unnecessary level of embarrassment for the leader of the council, number two lifted his hand slowly as a gesture for their guest to remain quiet. Then he looked at number one again and projected, "You are confused again my old friend. This has been a long council session and you are perhaps too tired to continue. If you will allow me, I can oversee the remainder of our brother's report. Please get some well-deserved rest, and I will locate you at a later time to brief you on what has transpired."

Turning toward number two, and then in the opposite direction to view a verifying nod from number three, the leader rose and removed himself from the proceedings. Then number two lowered his hand and projected to his brother below, "You suggested optimum results. Will you elaborate for us?"

While still confused by what had just transpired, he projected, "Members of the high council, it would appear that our original intent for the species of ₹-829-ᖇπ-3 may come to fruition after all. Some of those on the planet Earth as they refer to it have begun the transition. They have identified which among them possesses the ability, and they will nurture the offspring of those same individuals to grow strength in their numbers. Their evolutionary shift to the higher plane will take place rather quickly now, and that species ability to confront and over-come adversity should pay dividends for them in the future. We have achieved the ultimate goal of maintaining a portion of their species as they were, while also assisting in the creation of a hybrid variation of the humans."

Number two looked down upon his humble brother, then to his left and right. Each of the other members of the council had their eyes locked on their brother who had just given them the news. Then he returned his gaze forward and projected to all, "I don't believe there will be any need for deliberation on this matter. You have done well my brother, and speaking for those of the high council, we are pleased with how you have salvaged the situation with ₹-829-ᖇπ-3. Do you have anything else to add at this time?"

"Only that I thank you for the opportunity to serve."

"My brother, it is we who should be thanking you for what you have done. The exploratory fleet is honored to have you represent us in this matter, and the emperor will receive a positive report of this action on your behalf."

After bowing respectfully to each of the six members that remained, and glancing briefly at the empty chair in the middle position, he turned to exit the council chambers. Upon reaching the door, his escort projected, "Sir, it has been an honor presenting you to the high council on two occasions. If you will allow me, I believe that the next time you enter these chambers it will not be at the side of a security escort."

CHAPTER FORTY

THE LIFEBOAT

Minutes after their respective horizontal launches from the planet surface, escape velocity for the shuttles had once again been obtained without difficulty. Each of the sixteen specially redesigned spacecraft from the various population centers had set a course for a rendezvous with their recently completed mother ship in low Earth orbit over the northern magnetic pole. As with all of the numerous missions that had been necessary to first construct, and then fully equip the lifeboat throughout the previous two years, each of the shuttles would fit into docking clamps located along both sides of the mainframe. Within the course of that process, other than for the occasional observational need, there had never been more than half a dozen shuttles working on the lifeboat at any one time. The current endeavor was different however, and that would make the logistics of unloading their precious cargo during the vital final sequence more challenging. In this one and only instance, shuttles would be docking one after another while the remainder of the sixteen would engage in a delicate positioning dance in close proximity to the lifeboat.

It was well understood by each of the pilots and their right seat assistants that there was very little, if any, margin for error during that most hectic few hour time span. Unless there was some unforeseen problem causing a horrific accident, then each of the sixteen would dock only in their pre-determined sequence. The only exception to that would be if one or more of the spacecraft was either severely damaged or destroyed.

Hank gave a gentle nudge to the thrusters so that the Dripping Springs would remain at a safe distance from the Whitecliffs. The Maple Ridge was to Hank's port side, and was now closer than the Whitecliffs on his opposite beam, but he was less concerned with that proximity as a more experienced pilot was at the controls.

All three shuttles had been in a tight observational formation for more than an hour, while waiting for their turns within the sequence. Their time for docking had almost come, but Hank was still uneasy. He could tell that the pilot of the Whitecliffs was getting restless, and the continuing untidy motions of the spacecraft provided the proof. The fatigue that he faced could be magnified if his cargo within was also unsettled, and if that were the case, then the safety of all those around him could be in Jeopardy. A shuttle full of loud unruly children could make any pilot believe that minutes were more like hours, and therefore cause an uncorrectable distraction. Hank thought it unfortunate that the Maple Ridge would dock before either of them, but nothing could be done about that now. Hank would follow in the Dripping Springs, and then he would be blind to the actions of the frazzled pilot behind him.

Each of the eight shuttles designated to the port side of the ship had already docked, as had the first in the line of four lower tiered shuttles on the starboard side. As number ten in the progression, the Maple Ridge had just completed a smooth docking. Now during final approach to his assigned position, Hank made another fine-tuning adjustment with a gentle touch of the thrusters. A few seconds later, he saw the light on the instrument panel that indicated the docking clamps had locked the Dripping Springs into place. Turning to his assistant, Hank said, "Well then, that was easy enough. You did a good job of helping me with this flight, and your parents would have been proud of your effort."

Nicki, the now eleven year old daughter of Tori and Colt, was seated in the right-hand crew seat. Turning toward her mentor, she flashed him a thankful smile while beginning her post-flight checklist. She then replied, "I'm glad that I could help big brother, but it wouldn't have been possible if you hadn't taught me how to fly."

Hank knew that her training was incomplete, but a few of the Mayan's, including Tikal, had never really grasped the intricacies of flying the shuttle. When Hank had learned that Tori, and thus Nicki, were descendants of Ross, he wanted to ensure that she wasn't left behind on Earth with those who had not been chosen for the manifest. Hank knew that he needed an assistant for this one flight, so he provided Nicki with an accelerated training program in the hope that she would at least grasp some of the concepts.

Janet, although no longer angry with Tori or Colt, had been less than inspired by the thought at first. Even though the ancestral tie for Nicki with Ross obviously included Janet, she had never been part of the young girl's life. Nicki, like many other orphans, had been taken in by another family. Janet soon realized however that Nicki shouldn't be punished for having been a product of the gene enrichment program, and that she could also provide needed offspring for the colony several years from the present time. Beyond the now realized ancestral tie, Hank had also understood how difficult things had been for young Nicki when her mother had passed away. They also shared the loss of their common father Colt, and although Tori had been a nice person with a sharp intellect, Colt had been a more irreplaceable aspect of their life in Hank's opinion.

Hank returned the smile of his half-sister, and then mimicking the favorite verbal response of his earliest mentor, Megan Crenshaw, he said, "Well alright then. Let me help you with the post-flight checklist."

When they had completed their task, Hank locked out the ability for use of the control panel to anyone other than himself. He wanted to ensure that any youthful or untrained hands couldn't accidentally activate the panel while exploring what it had to offer during his absence.

Kristyn, seated next to her three younger half siblings projected, "What can I do to help Hank?"

His return thoughts were, "For the moment, just try to keep the little ones under control. We can't board until most of the others that arrived before us have finished shifting the food, water, and any equipment, that had been stored in their living quarters back into their now empty shuttles. It shouldn't be too long of a wait, but the scene inside the main body of the lifeboat would be chaotic if everyone was trying to accomplish that task at the same time."

"I understand, and with Janet's help, and Nicki if she wants to, I'm sure we can keep the little ones calm."

"Thanks Kristyn. Tikal and I can check on the progress of the other shuttles and their passengers, and we will return as soon as we can. Then we can begin to move everyone through the airlock into the habitat section of the lifeboat."

Within the course of the next two hours, each of the five remaining shuttles had safely clamped into a docking position without damaging any portion of the solar sails exterior masts or booms. Among those was the Whitecliffs, and they had, like their predecessors, also completed the process of transferring all of their human cargo onto the lifeboat. Each of them had carried a complement, including the pilot and an assistant, of twenty persons, and none had been reported as being injured from the events of the day. In total there were now three-hundred and twenty humans, with a mere twenty-eight of them being above the age of twelve, onboard the lifeboat and ready for the long traverse to Mars.

Of the non-human cargo that was moved back into the shuttles, the Whitecliffs had been pre-determined for use as one of the two that would house the vital greenhouse and the accompanying components of the hydroponic system. As such, that shuttle, along with the Crewe on the port side, would maintain a constant warm and inviting temperature by use of the onboard climate control system. Other shuttles would contain stores of food and water, and their temperature would be kept just a few degrees above freezing to ensure that nothing within them spoiled. The remaining shuttles would have no climate control until being initiated during the final few days of the journey, as attempting to protect equipment and machinery from the unrelenting icy cold of space would be a waste of precious power.

Every component of the lifeboat was now assembled in orbit, and there would be no returning to the confines of heavy gravity and the atmosphere below. Hank was relieved that there had been no damage done to the mainframe of the lifeboat or the docking clamps by any of the shuttles while completing final ascension, and he realized that at least that worrisome aspect of the voyage was behind them.

The time was now upon them to begin the much longer voyage away from Earth and its host star, but the first obstacle of the journey demanded focus and great care. The faint rings surrounding the planet that were comprised of small space rocks, iron ore composite, and ice would need to be safely navigated through with minimal impacts so as to not cause severe damage to the lifeboat. Looking up at them from Earth, the rings had been one element that created beautiful and awe inspiring sunrises and sunsets. Unfortunately for any spacecraft attempting to leave orbit, they created a potential navigational nightmare.

Hank and Joseph had been chosen to take the lifeboat out of orbit, and even though other pilots would rotate through the flight deck from time to time, those two men would be the primary crew for the duration of the voyage. Fortunately for them, the lifeboat, like the large airbuses of the early twenty-first century, would be on a computer automated flightpath for the majority of that time.

Assuming the left hand seat, Hank turned to Joseph in the right and said, "Shall we begin?"

"All set here. Are you ready to run the checklist?"

A few minutes later they had run through everything, and Hank said, "Alright then, let's take her straight up from the pole. That should keep us well clear of the majority of any orbiting ring debris."

"Roger that."

With that Hank pushed the throttles forward slightly, and pulled the wheel toward him. The only sense of movement that could be felt was by looking through the large forward glass, as the planet that had been in view quickly dropped below them. The multiple bands of rings then passed from the top to the bottom of their view, and nothing but a vast field of unexplored stars, at least by the humans, could be seen. Once clear of any fragments of the outer most ring debris field, the exact course needed to intercept the orbiting path of Mars at a fixed point was entered into the onboard computer. A substantial amount of lead time would be necessary in order to match the speed and trajectory of not only their intended target, but the inner most of her two orbiting moons. Unlike the oceangoing vessels of Earth's yesteryear that simply set a course for a stationary land mass, the lifeboat needed to be aimed with exacting precision at an empty point in space that Mars would briefly occupy in several months. Hopefully, if all the calculations were correct, the end result would be a triumphant rendezvous with Earths neighboring red marble in space. If not, then the lifeboat would simply drift on through the darkness with no chance of long term survival.

Hank had remembered Ross once informing him that the scientists of his earlier life on Earth had calculated a six month voyage would be necessary in order to reach Mars. That calculation during the days of NASA had been based primarily on two factors. First were the available propulsion systems that the technology of those years had provided, while the second relied on the respective orbits of each planet and their optimum positions to each other at the time of launch. Unfortunately, neither of those calculable factors could be replicated for the current endeavor.

What was known about NASA from the historical disks, or from the various probes which had been discovered and retrieved from Mars, was a constant mind set with regard to the speed of flight. The unmanned probes sent to Mars by NASA, or other space agencies of the time, had used a propulsion system that generated identical velocity throughout the duration of the journey. Fortunately, a more advanced system of propulsion had been developed by the scientific community of new Earth that would allow for a steady increase of speed, and its use had already been successfully proven with modern day probes.

That technological advancement would have made the upcoming journey a more palatable duration of four months, but Mars was not currently in the optimum orbital position to do so. As the red planet requires slightly less than twice as long to orbit the sun as the Earth does, the Earth is perpetually either pulling ahead of, or catching up to, as in the current case, the position of Mars. It was not possible to remain on Earth waiting for optimal positioning, so the truth became inescapable. One of the aforementioned factors would be most favorable, while the other would be a significant detriment. Even with the aid of the six energy collecting and velocity enhancing solar sails that would soon be deployed, the journey to Mars, or ₹-829-4 as their old alien friends referred to it, would require eight full months to complete.

CHAPTER FORTY-ONE

ARRIVAL

Tikal entered the flight deck area of the lifeboat where Hank and Joseph sat at the controls. After gazing out the large viewing window he projected, "It looks bigger than it did a few days ago when we collapsed those sail things."

Hank replied in kind, "You mean the solar sails that we used to get here? By collapsing them we have halted the slow and steady acceleration process that had been building up over the past eight months. Since furling all six of them in, we have been gliding at a constant speed. As for Mars, yes it looks much larger, and isn't she beautiful?"

"Yes it is beautiful, but why did you call it she?"

"Ross told me once, and Joseph among others has confirmed it, that long ago on Earth many lifeless objects of beauty such as cars, ships, or planes were often referred to as she. I thought that I would pay Mars the same level of respect."

"I'm not familiar with any of those objects that you're referring to Hank, but if you feel the need to label that thing out there as a she, then go ahead."

"Thanks Tikal, I will."

"Janet informed me that I should come see you, as you have some information that could be interesting."

Pointing toward a barely discernable white mass at the left of Mars, Hank replied, "Yes I do Tikal. That little white blob is Diemos. It's the outer most of the two moons. Soon we will see the inner moon Phobos, which is nearly twice the size, and then we can begin our breaking procedure."

Having learned from Ross of the "slingshot" model used for acceleration purposes by numerous probes during the space age that predated the apocalypse, Hank thought something similar might be of use for this vessel. During the early stages of development for the lifeboat, he presented his concept to what remained of the scientific brain trust. They in turn developed a method to reverse that process by ingeniously using the small amount of gravity created by Phobos to gently grab hold of the lifeboat as it passed close by. The intent would be to slow down the craft by having it circle the small moon several times, and then the vessel would move toward Mars where the remainder of the breaking procedure could be handled by much larger gravitational forces. After a few revolutions of the red planet, a controlled descent to the region of the northern polar ice cap could commence.

Gazing at the small white blob of Diemos, Tikal then projected, "Hank, do you really think that this will work?"

"It should. I'm aware that no one from the team who developed the plan lived long enough to come with us, but they explained how everything worked to me and a few of the other pilots long before we left Earth."

"You just informed me that we were headed for the northern ice cap of the planet?"

"Yes. Many of the probes that were sent during the ancient time of NASA, and all of those launched in more recent years, revealed that the northern ice cap is significantly larger than its sister at the southern pole."

"Sister?"

"Sorry. That's just another one of those old Earth expressions that Ross told me about. Anyway, as we can now plainly see, the information from each of those probes was correct. Besides, that's where the cave chambers are."

"So when do we get there?"

"If all goes according to the plan, then it should only be a couple more days."

"That's good. I can't wait to get off of this vessel and really stretch my legs."

"That won't be as easy as you think. First I must put this lifeboat down in exactly the right place, and then a few of us in pressurized spacesuits will need to do a lot of work before you or anyone else can simply move about underground."

Two days later Hank activated the controls that would allow the lifeboat to begin an orbit around Phobos. To his knowledge, no one among the passengers even noticed the change in pitch angle, as the small moon caused the vessel to bank ever so slightly to port. While adjusting the controls set forth by the flight operational specifications, Hank smiled as the gauges revealed a slight slowing of the vessels momentum.

Standing proudly behind him was Janet, and after Hank gave her a quick smiling glance, she projected, "It must be working."

Hank returned the projection of, "Yes it is. So far the drop in our speed is less than one percent, but at least we know the concept works. I don't expect that the small body of Phobos will have a tremendous impact in decreasing our speed, but anything will help. It also gives me greater confidence that we can achieve a safe descent speed to the surface after our planned deceleration orbits around Mars."

"You mean you didn't have ultimate confidence in this theory until now. Why didn't you tell me?"

"Of course I had confidence in the theory. The people who developed the process were not only very smart, but all of the specifics looked fantastic on paper. What I meant was that now the theory has been tested through practical application, and actually experiencing the results, no matter how minute, have increased my belief in the overall success of the plan."

Hank was aware, at perhaps a much greater level than Janet, that the entire venture was a long shot at best. Even if the aspect of the lifeboat landing was successful, there was no guarantee that the human contingent could survive in the long term. However, he was also aware that a distinguishable level of belief in the overall success of their quest existed within the youthful population. Such a belief could become significant when it came time to persevere over unforeseen obstacles in their future. If all did go according to the complex plan, then their efforts would ensure that the alien species would need to reclassify the red planet as ₹-829-ʊπ-4. The addition of ʊπ would signify that life with an aptitude for both language and math now existed on the planet.

CHAPTER FORTY-TWO

THE RED CAVITY

As expected, the completion of the process had taken three months for those few who could actually perform the necessary work, but the challenge of the vital and daunting task performed entirely while in pressurized spacesuits had been met. A series of cave chambers under the northern ice cap had been discovered, and subsequently mapped, through the use of sensors from exploratory probes before the lifeboat ever left Earth orbit, and the newly completed portal toward them was now believed to be fully secure.

That painstaking process had begun from a location beneath the underbelly of the lifeboat within hours after their arrival on the Martian surface. After Hank had manipulated the thrusters of the lifeboat to expertly navigate through a valley framed by long fingers of the thick ice cap, he successfully set the ship down within meters of the hopeful pre-determined landing site. That snug location between towering fields of ice at the valleys termination point would not only help protect the ship from any conditions that the Martian surface and limited atmosphere might create, but it was also in close proximity to one of the larger discovered sub-surface cave chambers. With each of the onboard systems checked, and all sections of the lifeboat deemed to be secure, Hank suited up. Descending through the forward airlock for his initial extravehicular stroll, Hank then instantly joined a very select group of individuals. He had just become the modern day version of Neil Armstrong, or what his own older half-brother Ross had originally believed himself to be, as the first member of the human species to set foot on a world other than Earth. Shortly after that historic moment, which would never be recognized by anyone other than the group of survivors within the lifeboat, a handful of the Mayan men and women joined him on the surface of Mars. Hank knew that there would be no time for any celebration or ceremony for having done so, as any such action could, and most assuredly should, wait until after all the upcoming work had been completed. Not being one of those people who clamored for notoriety, he quickly made peace with that truth. For him, it was actually more gratifying to know how successful he had been with the landing.

The deep access tunnel to the cave chambers, which in the most simplest of terms demanded total success, had then been dug through the rocky soil of the Martian landscape. That process, which included shoring up the perimeter walls and ceiling against potential collapse, required removing most of the excavation tailings. Those tailings were subsequently utilized as several feet of compacted insulation within four constructed walls reaching from the planet surface to the smooth underbelly of the lifeboat. Once those had been erected, and thoroughly inspected for sound structural integrity, the entire surface of each wall, both inside and out, were then sprayed with the same honey like substance that had been used to seal the joints along the external and internal shells of the lifeboat. An airtight seal against the minimal Martian atmosphere had thusly been achieved, and in time that fully enclosed area surrounding the tunnel entrance would enable the human cargo to transition both to and from the lifeboat and the caves with the upmost of safety. As additional sections of the tunnel were completed, that same invisible lining had been applied in order to seal any of the fissures in the rock strata that might create venting to the surface high above. When the tunnel reached the large cave chambers, much of the loose soil that remained from the dig was moved into positions within where food would soon be cultivated.

With the tunnel completed, work then began to ensure the structural integrity and sealing of the chambers along with the preparation for occupation. Several small bore holes were drilled through the ceiling and into the lower levels of the thick ice cap above. Their purpose was vital for life within the caves, as the holes would provide a water source needed not only for the everyday needs of drinking water, but to also satisfy the perpetual thirst of the food growing hydroponic system. When the people inhabited the caves, they would actually aid in that process. Their numerous daily activities, and cumulative body heat, would create enough rising warm air through the bore holes to allow for a slow melting of the ice. Even with that action, it was believed that the overall thickness of the polar cap would never be jeopardized. The constant and unrelenting icy cold of space would ensure that the exposed outer layer would forever remain intact.

Finally, before the climactic phase of relocating the people, supplies, and any needed equipment into the caves could commence, one more task needed to be performed. A steady stream of fresh oxygen would need to be pumped through the portal tunnel and into the cave chambers from the processors aboard the lifeboat. Those processors had done an admirable job of providing the compliment of passengers with the life sustaining gas throughout the long eight month voyage from Earth, and the additional three months since the landing, but now their capabilities would be further stretched.

When the ultimate moment of truth arrived for the final test, Hank stood alone within the main chamber. Taking a deep breath, he thought of all those who had sacrificed so this entire desperate attempt, and this specific moment, could be realized. Then he projected, "Can you hear me?"

Janet, perhaps projecting for the collective replied, "Yes we can hear you Hank. How's it going in there?"

"Everything is fine, so you might as well start pushing the oxygen through whenever you are ready."

On the flight deck of the lifeboat, Janet gave the signal to one of the other pilots to begin the process. Then she projected only to Hank, "I hope this works."

Gazing in anticipation at the sensor gauge in his hand, Hank replied, "So do I mom, so do I. If all goes according to specifications, then I should get a positive read for oxygen in just a few minutes."

For the next fifteen minutes, those on the flight deck remained silent while waiting for a report from Hank. Although there were expressions of concern on their faces during the lengthy silence, it would serve no purpose to pester him with idle projected chatter. Within the cave, Hank had been moving around to several locations, while comparing the corresponding readings of the sensor gauge. When he reached the back wall of a small chamber located furthest from the tunnel entrance, he stopped. A moment later a smile rose on his face as the gauge began to register positively.

Unable to wait any longer for an overdue report, Janet broke the silence with, "Hank, are you there?"

Somewhat perturbed, he projected, "Yes mom, I'm still here. Where else would I be?"

"Don't behave like your father. What's happening?"

"It's good news. The levels vary at different locations within the chambers, but the sensor gauge is detecting oxygen."

"Wonderful. How soon do you think we can begin the moving process?"

"That's difficult to answer at this time."

"Why? Is there a problem?"

"I don't think so, but some of the oxygen readings are still very low. It could take several hours before each of the various chambers has readings that are suitable, and we don't want to push the processors too hard."

"I understand, but everyone has been cooped up for a long time. They are all anxious to have a larger habitat to move about in."

"I realize that mom, but moving everyone into these chambers at the same time could be dangerous. Consider what all of their movement, and the obvious excitement level that would accompany it, could do too many of them as they attempt to claim a spot to call their own. It's important to maintain the delicate atmospheric balance that has been established, and in order to do that we need to ensure that a controlled and disciplined entry is carried out. If we can't accomplish that, then the majority of the available oxygen in here could be used up before the processors can replenish it. After all that we have been through, we don't want our people gasping for air just moments after moving in here do we?"

CHAPTER FORTY-THREE

THE FLAG OF OPTIMISM

The day after his initial oxygen test within the cave chambers, Hank suited up once more for a descent through the forward airlock. Once down inside the tunnel, he realized that an artificial atmosphere of oxygen existed. Although Hank had not yet activated the sensor device, he could feel the heaviness of additional gravity. Having worked for three months on the tunnel and cave chambers while in gravity that was only thirty-eight percent of that which existed on Earth, Hank had become an expert on how easily one could move about while in a pressurized spacesuit. Now those same movements became more labored for him, and there could only be one explanation as to the change.

After checking several locations within the chambers, and projecting the now acceptable, although less than ideal, oxygen readings for each of those positions to Janet on the flight deck, he added, "Should I proceed with the final test?"

"Based on your readings, the air will be rather thin much like that of very high altitude areas of Earth. But if you are ready to proceed, then go ahead."

Smiling with anticipation, Hank loosened the locking clasp and slowly opened the face shield of his helmet. Then he continued to breathe normally, and even drew in more deeply several times with no apparent ill effects. A moment later, he projected, "The air is colder than I thought it would be, and very thin as you believed, but it's definitely breathable."

"Excellent. Do you want to take the next step?"

"Sure, I'm going to need to do that eventually."

"That's true. Proceed whenever you're ready Hank."

"Alright then, here we go."

With an ever broadening smile, Hank reached up to pull the helmet off and away from his head. Then he removed his gloves before commencing a leisurely, and for what would be the final time, a solitary stroll throughout the main chamber. While doing so, he formed a visual picture within his mind of what would transpire. The peacefulness that he now enjoyed would soon be replaced by teeming activity, and the often loud and undisciplined verbal utterances of the children. Given time though, that chaotic reality would morph into an entirely different way of life. Those who had not yet begun the process of the evolutionary shift would eventually do so, as they would receive the occasional fragmented thought. From there, the transformation into the higher plane of non-verbal telepathic communication for the entire colony would happen quickly.

Suddenly his thoughts were interrupted as he heard a projection from his mother. "Hank, are you there?"

Feeling somewhat perturbed by the foolish question, he replied, "Of course I'm here, where else would I be?"

"Hank, we have been through this before. Please don't behave like that. Now is everything alright?"

"Yes, everything is fine in here. I'm heading back to the lifeboat, and we can begin preparations for the first group."

The hours and days of transition that followed went more smoothly than Hank initially believed they would, and with regard to his preconceived notion, he was happy to be proved incorrect. In time, each of the colonists settled into their own particular patterns of behavior. People performed the tasks, pleasant or otherwise, that were necessary to keep the collective alive. The hydroponic system, enabled by the planned ice melt through the bore holes above, had continued to provide through the growth of life sustaining food. A small exercise area that had been installed on the lifeboat continued to provide, as it had done throughout the voyage from Earth, by harnessing the energy created via pedal power. The vents along portions of the exterior shell that led to the turbines, and the forward two deployed solar sails on the lifeboat, had also provided a useful amount of power. By collecting wind that existed within the atmosphere which had funneled into the canyons between the walls of ice, and the distant rays of their host star, every aspect of the old SSP vehicle had been brought to bear.

Then in what seemed to be the blink of an eye, four months of Earth time had passed without incident. Now a year since their departure from Earth, and seemingly without notice, the much anticipated moment for Kristyn was suddenly upon them. Aided by two Mayan women, each of whom had been on the opposite side of the process three separate times while on Earth, she labored through the pain. Many of those within the nearby chambers patiently waited for the outcome, as Hank nervously paced with far less of it while in front of Joseph. Soon a slap, and the ensuing cry, could be heard by all, as Kristyn had given birth to Hank's child.

Within the group of female colonists, she had been the obvious choice for all those who had been paying any level of attention. Hank and Kristyn may not have known initially, but as they grew older they eventually came to realize that the two of them had been visualized by Ross and several others as an eventual mating pair from the very beginning of the gene enrichment program. Although it was true that the long term plan had called for Hank and Kristyn to create children from multiple mates, something about their early friendship and the way they interacted toward one another made some believe that they were destined for the long haul. Even her mother Natiya had seen the light from early on, as they were the only two of their age group on the initial voyage from ₹-593-૨π-2-2. Now within this current group of three-hundred and twenty souls that had braved the necessary trip to Mars, Hank and Kristyn, now twenty-one and twenty respectfully, proved that they belonged together more so than ever before.

As for the other females within the collective, only the ten Mayan women, now ranging from thirty-two through forty, and Brittany at thirty-eight, maintained a level of physiological development that would allow for childbearing. Although each were still quite able to conceive, all eleven of them had previously bore, at a minimum, two children for the gene enrichment program during their time on Earth. A few of their respective daughters, and other young ladies that included Nicki, Kristyn's two younger sisters, and Joseph's daughter, were quickly approaching the phase of their life cycle that would enable them to contemplate reproduction. In reality though, Janet and others understood that the practicality of their use for such purposes would still be several years away. Aside from the obvious strain it would place on their bodies at such an early age, there was the emotional level of their development to consider. As that aspect of life didn't generally progress at the same pace as the maturity of their bodies, a young lady in her early teens shouldn't be required, especially given the adaptation process to their new environment that each was experiencing, with the responsibility of childbirth.

Seeing Hank move toward her and their newborn son, Kristyn smiled and projected, "Well it wasn't easy, but I did it."

Returning a broad smile he replied to her joyful projection with, "You most certainly did Kristyn, and I will be forever grateful. We have just become the parents of the first human being to be born on Mars!"

As one of the Mayan midwives moved closer with the item that the proud parents had chosen for use as the baby blanket, Hank rubbed the emblem attached to the thin chain around his neck and flashed back to a distant fond memory of when Ross had introduced him to a young girl named Kristyn. Then his thoughts were interrupted, as the now cloaked baby boy was handed to him. Cradling the infant in his arms, he looked at Kristyn and projected, "What do you think we should name him?"

"I think that we should name him Ross."

"Ross? That's very sweet of you, but why?"

"There are so many reasons Hank, including the fact that he had the vision long ago of putting the two of us together, but I think that there is one reason that stands clear above the rest."

"What's that?"

"It just seems fitting that Ross should be the name of the first child born during the course of this endeavor to ensure that our species, however we may have and will evolve, does not die out."

Smiling at the sentiment, Hank gazed down upon his newborn son. He was securely wrapped in the American flag that centuries before had briefly occupied the oval office within the White House during the administration of the man whom he had just been named after. The faded and tattered flag removed from the Cheyenne Mountain museum complex fit baby Ross well, and Hank was overjoyed. Then after a quick glance in Kristyn's direction, he projected proudly, "Well hello there Ross, it's nice to meet you."

Hank knew the smile that then appeared on his son's little precious face was most assuredly coincidental, but with the genetics of two telepathic parents working in his favor, perhaps little Ross had heard his father's projection.

Then Kristyn projected, "Hey Hank, do you ever think about how all of the people back on our old home moon are doing?"

ꝓ

CHAPTER FORTY-FOUR

THE RITE OF PASSAGE

The alien who had unintentionally made contact with Ross long ago on the surface of Earths now extinct moon, and then subsequently became his respected friend and mentor, now stood for the first time next to the marked graves of Ross and all of those who had either been close friends or members of his family. Although saddened by the reality of what the site represented, and those of the several hundred other nearby human burial mounds, the alien was pleased to have been afforded the opportunity for a moment of quiet reflection before his upcoming meeting.

Having been the key player in an odyssey which had enabled the human species of ₹-829-ૐπ-3 to avoid possible extinction on their home world, the alien had been ordered to report back to where it all began. That order had come to him shortly after his most recent audience with the high council, and had been issued by an even higher authority. Now, with the entourage approaching, he turned toward them and bowed his head. As a show of unwavering respect, his intent was to remain in that humble posture until given permission to do otherwise. A moment later, he received a telepathic message requesting that he look up, and having done so, he then resisted the urge to bow down once again. The ageing and frail high emperor of his species upon the home world, and all of those who had colonized different worlds, now stood directly in front of his obedient subject. Then with a faint smile on his face, the emperor projected a message of, "You have achieved excellent results with regard to this most delicate project brother, and in the process you have represented the exploratory fleet and our species with lofty distinction. I would like to discuss how you devised such a masterful plan?"

Gazing upon the face of his supreme leader for the first time, the alien returned the telepathy with a humble, "Thank you very much for your kind thoughts emperor. Of course it would be my honor to discuss anything that you wish."

Placing an outstretched hand on the shoulder of his subject, the emperor projected, "This is the first time that I have visited system ₹-829. My assistant has informed me that we are now standing on the third planet, and that the former dominant species had a special classification for it."

"Yes emperor, this is the third planet from the host star within this system. Long ago it was charted and then classified in our data base as ₹-829-ૐπ-3, but the species of humans that once lived here referred to it as Earth."

"Earth? They used a word in place of a number. That's a strange way to classify a planet."

"Yes it is emperor, but like many of the planets or moons that we have charted, there was no real need for the inhabitants of them to identify solar systems with numbers. I have learned from my human friend Ross that for the majority of their history, his species lived in denial that any world other than their own ever existed. In fact, many Earth centuries ago, before Ross became one of their species leaders, the arrogant human belief of singularity went far beyond that. For a brief instant during the dawn of their scientific knowledge, the human species actually believed that their host star revolved around their home planet!"

"All of those facts have been well documented in our data base via the many reports that your predecessors filed with fleet operations."

"Yes emperor. And as I then documented within my reports, when human science finally advanced to an elementary level enabling the discovery of other planets within this system, then names were given to classify them as well."

"Indeed. So that rather strange custom of theirs goes beyond this world. Can you provide me with a more detailed accounting of those classifications?"

"Yes emperor, I can. Before the asteroid had impacted and destroyed Earths singular moon, the planet closest to the host star was known as Mercury. The second had been given the name of Venus, while the nearest of an outward position from Earth was called Mars. The four much larger planets that comprise the outer reaches of the system are Jupiter, Saturn, Uranus and Neptune. For an instant in human history there was another beyond those four named Pluto, but the humans discovered that the orbiting body was not actually a planet."

"Those are all very strange classifications. Do you know if each one has a specific meaning?"

"Yes emperor, they do. Ross also informed me that each was the name of a deity within the mythological structure of an ancient culture on Earth."

"Indeed. It's interesting that a species on the verge of serious exploration beyond their own world would place that much importance on deities."

"Yes emperor, but those names were given to each of the planets several centuries of Earth time before the humans had the technological ability to venture into space. What's really interesting to me is that the knowledge of such names had not faded away from their collective memory during the twenty-six Earth centuries that had passed since the most recent of large asteroid impacts. That information is also well documented within the more recent of my reports to fleet operations, but when Ross learned of this upon his return to Earth he was pleasantly surprised."

"Surprised? Could you explain that please?"

"Well emperor. For Ross, as one of the select few members of his species to actually venture into space before our efforts to relocate him and others to ₹-593-ॐπ-2-2, the planets of this system represented something larger than the deities they were named for. The neighboring planets are the logical first step in deeper space exploration, and his species was on the verge of a manned mission to one of them before the incoming asteroid altered their priorities. Even though the surviving human population of Earth's apocalyptic event then quickly dismissed the belief structure of deities for their daily existence, they did maintain a respect for the names of such entities given to celestial bodies. Ross understood that their new found realization of self-reliance and accountability for each individual's own fate, coupled with the acknowledgement and respect for an ancient cultural belief system, represented a small but important evolutionary step for his species. Each of those brave enlightenments had helped put an end to many of the childish and selfish behaviors that nearly led to the demise of their own cherished species. He admired the advances that had occurred upon the world that he returned to, and as a byproduct of those advances, the lack of various uncontrollable problems that had existed on the Earth of his youthful years. It also gave Ross comfort to know that he would spend his final days of mortal life here on his birth world, and I'm glad that he could finally rest easy."

Glancing down at the small plot of land where Ross had been placed for that well-deserved rest, the emperor removed his outstretched hand from the shoulder of his subject. Then he confirmed the thoughts of his brother, "I agree with your sentiment. Based on previous information, and what you have just conveyed, that human was a positive example of his species and a respected leader among them."

"Yes emperor, he was. But he was not the only one of their species to show such promise."

"That's good to know brother, as it speaks well for their future in the galactic equation."

"Yes emperor, I believe so too."

Turning from the gravesite, the Emperor changed the subject of their conversation by projecting, "As to how this planet could benefit the long term goal of our species, I think that it's time for the two of us to discuss the intricacies of your overall plan."

"Yes emperor. As you know, we had been observing many forms of life on this planet throughout several of their known centuries, and on three occasions had seen fit to relocate a small amount of them to ₹-593-ᴣπ-2-2. Many of those species of life on this planet showed minimal, if any, evolutionary progress during that time span. However, the humans had in many ways emerged as the one truly dominant species. In the latter stages of our observations their abilities from a technological standpoint had advanced very quickly. Unfortunately that so called advancement created a growing concern within our observation teams. The humans could have easily destroyed themselves, and nearly every other species of life present on this planet, before they evolved philosophically."

"Indeed. Unfortunately there have been examples of that type of behavior on other worlds. The extinction of any species results in a loss of strength with regard to the galactic community, but a self-inflicted extinction that may also cause other species to perish is significantly tragic!"

"Yes emperor, and in the case of ₹-829-ᴣπ-3, the human species were closer to such a fate than many of them believed. Not only did they identify the vast majority of other lifeforms on their world as insignificant, but they also had a tendency to treat others of their own species as inferior. There were a minimal percentage of the humans who could visualize the broader scope and cherished it, but most just existed in blissful arrogance. They continued to develop more efficient ways of killing each other, and invented new reasons to do exactly that. For the most part they all had a deep burning desire to live, but had absolutely no problem with doing so at the expense of others of their own kind. In addition to those problems, they were consuming their natural resources at an alarming rate while also polluting their atmosphere and water beyond livable conditions. At that moment of their history, their future was extremely doubtful."

"Once again, those are facts that have been well documented in the reports that you and your predecessors filed with fleet operations."

"Yes emperor, but that was when we began to monitor their world more closely. In spite of that general absence of moral and philosophical fiber, the human species did show a level of promise that they could belong to a larger galactic community. Although gradual at first, more and more of their species began to believe that additional planets and moons, with perhaps other lifeforms grander than their own, could actually exist somewhere else in the universe. Then a segment of their developing technology and resources were actually dedicated to exploring such a possibility, but those resources were minor when compared to all that had been dedicated toward the problems that I mentioned."

"Indeed. So you are claiming that their developing technology led them to the brink, and that they then teetered between extinction and enlightenment because of it."

"Yes emperor they did, and then forces well beyond even our control entered the equation."

"Indeed. The mysteries of the universe can do that."

"Yes emperor. We, as the potential guardians of their plight, were suddenly faced with a challenging situation. By all logic, their world was about to be destroyed by the impact of a massive asteroid, but our belief structure is to save a species whenever possible. Even though a minute percentage of their species was living on ₹-593-Ʒπ-2-2, they were decedents of Earth's more ancient civilizations. It was unclear if members of their current technologically advanced society could coexist with them, but there was no other available option. Besides, from an observational standpoint it created a tremendous opportunity to monitor their evolutionary process. With that in mind we offered a small segment of their population an opportunity to relocate to another world, but we didn't inform them that other members of their species were already living upon it until we completed the transport."

"Was that when you devised your brilliant plan?"

"No emperor. At that point in time we had no idea if this planet would retain its overall mass integrity. Even if it didn't violently shake into crumbled bits, we weren't sure if any atmosphere would exist in the aftermath of the asteroid collision with the orbiting moon and the bombardment of chunks from both bodies onto the surface. Consequently, the thought of Earth as a possible colonization site was never considered. Reports show that it took several centuries of human time-line before the planet cleansed itself enough to entertain the idea of our species living upon it. Unfortunately, our closer inspection at that time revealed that we once again faced a challenge. Although their population was limited, the human species had somehow survived and exhibited traits of having evolved to a higher philosophical plane. Their actions suggested that they had learned to live and work together in total harmony, which was vastly different than the way their species had generally behaved toward one another throughout the centuries leading up to the apocalypse. In essence, the human species had showed our species positive signs that the shift in their evolution could still occur, it just needed a little help along the way."

"That must have been a difficult test for you, as your decisions and subsequent actions would seriously impact the future of both ours and the human species."

"Yes emperor, it was difficult for me from an ethical viewpoint, but not logistically. I developed my plan when we learned that the human genetic code on this planet was in serious peril. Without the plan, it would have been necessary to wait another human century, or perhaps even slightly longer. They would have reached the point of total genetic collapse very shortly, but I found a way to correct that issue."

"Indeed, and your plan was brilliant in its conception. You have successfully and peaceably eradicated this planet of what remained of the dominant species, while also ensuring that they had the opportunity to survive by stretching their technological and philosophical abilities. More importantly, you accomplished that delicate process without using force in order to do so."

"Thank you emperor, that's very kind of you."

"Your actions on this world have impressed the high council of our exploratory fleet, and they have provided me with a recommendation. I'm pleased to inform you that I'm in total agreement with their assessment. Although it's true that both you and your father led past observational formations involving this planet that ended badly with the loss of a scout ship and its personnel, those former indiscretions have been forgiven. As of now, your family name has been cleared by me at the recommendation of the high council. Additionally, I'm presenting you with a well-deserved field promotion to the position of administrator of colonization for this planet."

Somewhat in awe of the news, the alien projected, "Thank you very much emperor. That's wonderful news about my family name, and it's also a tremendous honor for me to receive this promotion. I shall do my best to serve you and our species with distinction throughout the future colonization process."

"I know that you will, and there may be more to follow for you when that colonization process is complete. Now then, I must ask you one question. How did you develop the plan of introducing a slowly gestating deadly virus into their population base for the eradication process?"

"To be honest emperor, I didn't devise the plan in that fashion. I wanted to ensure that either their species or ours, whichever was the most resilient, would inhabit and thrive on this blue planet. If the human species could adapt to what had been brought, inadvertently or otherwise, from ₹-593-ᴣᴜπ-2-2, then so be it. The infusion of fresh genetic code represented within Ross's group of recruits had the potential to assure their long term survival here on ₹-829-ᴣᴜπ-3. Because a certain number of them possessed the untapped ability of telepathy, they could reinvigorate the telepathic evolutionary shift that had been stalled for several centuries. However, if the normally benign virus of ₹-593-ᴣᴜπ-2-2 that Ross and others carried with them became something their species could not adapt to, as was proven to be the case, then no harm would have actually been done. As noted in several reports, the human presence on this planet already faced a very limited future. In either of the two scenarios, our species would have kept to our core belief system of giving life on a galactic scale a fighting chance. I will freely admit that the ultimate result of the endeavor was unexpected, as both of our species will profit. We will be able to colonize this planet to help secure our future, and those few remaining human survivors that are experiencing an evolution shift into a hybrid species will prosper as well. They have escaped what became a deadly virus for them on their home world of Earth, and have ventured into space to begin anew."

"That's all true, but I don't really expect those few humans to survive. Although they have made a brave attempt to be sure, they can't possibly journey to another star system. The spacecraft that they have constructed, and the antiquated propulsion system that it contains, would need centuries of their timeline to reach even the closest neighboring star."

"That's true emperor, but their species has no intention at this point in time of leaving this solar system. Perhaps you are unaware, but they set a course to rendezvous with ₹-829-4, and successfully landed there roughly five of their Earth years ago. After departure, their transit took less than one of their years to complete, and since that time they have forged out an existence by developing an underground colony."

"₹-829-4? Do you mean that neighboring red planet that is nearly the same size as this one?"

"Yes emperor. The historical documents from our long ago observations provide evidence that the planet contained life at some point in the distant past. Now a small group of stubbornly determined and resilient humans, who once resided here on ₹-829-ᴣ∪π-3, have reestablished life upon it."

"But that can't be. Our current research indicates that the minimal atmosphere of the red planet is not compatible with their species needs. They most surely would have quickly perished without the ability to create a suitable atmosphere."

"That would have been true in the past emperor, but please don't assume that they have no chance. The human species continues to show me an amazing resilience to an array of obstacles that they have encountered. We must respect the fact that they have made a bold attempt to not only colonize another planet, but to embrace and continue to strive toward their destined evolutionary shift in the process. The hybrid humans, if it's not too bold of me to label them as such, have taken on a daunting challenge on ₹-829-4, while at the same time leaving a few members of their species here to eventually perish. Although they are unaware of exactly when it occurred, the last of their kind died a few of their months ago. Forgive me emperor, but no, we can't count them out. The transitional leap of mind and body that they took to another world was accomplished while seeking only minimal assistance from us to ensure the structural stability of their spacecraft for the journey. Then they sought no additional assistance beyond using that same sealing compound while establishing a suitable habitat once they arrived. Although it's true that the odds were against them from the very beginning, the effort on their part has provided proof that the hybrid humans do not wish to perish as a species. All that they seek is the opportunity for a continued and prosperous evolution of life, and as I mentioned previously, they are extremely determined. For that reason alone emperor, I would like to request that we now officially reclassify that little red planet of theirs as ₹-829-ꝋπ-4."

Realizing the passion with which his humble brother had conveyed his thoughts, and the general concern for the ultimate goal of enhancing their species existence while also preserving others, the emperor felt he could now endorse the subsequent recommendation that had been presented to him by the exploratory fleet's high council. Accordingly, he gave a final projection of, "You have shown me great promise for the future, and I will reward you because of it. When you have completed your duties with the preliminary aspects and initial colonization of this planet, another task awaits you."

"I understand emperor, and what is that task?"

"It is beyond the time when the leader of the high council should have stepped down, but that will take effect upon my return to the home world. I had known for quite some time that he maintained a grudge against your family name, as one within his family died during the observational formation led by your father. Number two shall ascend, and in so doing it has been suggested by that body that you should receive the entry position of number seven upon the high council. I once again concur with the belief of those who reside upon it, and ask that you accept my offer to join them and bring forth your wisdom to the bench?"

After a step backwards in disbelief, the alien bowed deeply and then projected, "On behalf of my father, who also gave his life on this planet near a place that the humans called Roswell during the pre-apocalyptic Earth year of 1947, I thank you emperor. It would be my pleasure to continue serving you and the exploratory fleet by accepting the great honor that you have bestowed upon my family."

CHAPTER FORTY-FIVE
THE FUTURE VOICE

On ₹-829-३ᴜπ-4, or Mars as the hybrid humans living there preferred to call it, Hank and Ross had just heard the latest cry to signify the birth of another colonist. Ross, now eight years old, rubbed the emblem on the necklace that his father had recently presented to him, and thought about those few who had cherished the item before him. Upon Kristyn's return from assisting with the delivery, Hank projected to her, is everything alright?"

"Yes, Nicki and the baby are fine. How is Ross doing?"

"Well, I haven't heard any response, so I don't believe that his message got through."

Kristyn nodded and then projected, "Ross, your father and I would like you to try again please."

"Alright mom, I'll give it another try."

The ensuing look upon Ross's face reveled that he was properly focused on the effort, and back on ₹-829-३ᴜπ-3, the administrator of colonization heard a faint projection. The telepathic message was short and sweet, but it spoke volumes. "Hello, can you hear me? My name is Ross, and my parents and grandmother have told me that you are a friend of theirs."

ABOUT THE AUTHOR

Kurt possesses a spirit of adventure, which drives his thirst for experiencing new places and activities. He maintains a love for the great outdoors, and enjoys traveling whenever his schedule permits. One of his favorite activities is hiking in the clean mountain air, where the tranquil locations provide him with an opportunity to develop characters and storylines for his books. Kurt currently resides in Northern Nevada, where he and his wife have lived for more than a decade.

CPSIA information can be obtained
at www.ICGtesting.com
Printed in the USA
FSHW021036220719
60266FS